D1795972

SEDELLA

THE STORY OF A SPANISH VILLAGE

JOHN HARDY

Text copyright

© John Hardy 2016

Back cover photograph

© Francisco Santiago
Guirado 2016

All rights reserved

BOOKS BY JOHN HARDY

MALAGA MYSTERIES
TWISTED TALES
ANDALUCÍAN MYSTERIES
MORE ANDALUCÍAN MYSTERIES
EAST SIDE STORIES
6.10 FROM DARLINGTON (SHORT STORY)
THE OTHONA VALEDICTION (3 SHORT STORIES)
DOUBLE JEOPARDY (SHORT STORY)
SEDELLA - THE STORY OF A SPANISH VILLAGE

WITH HEIKE VAGEN:
ANDALUSISCHE GESCHICHTEN

WITH ISABEL PÉREZ:
MISTERIOS DE ANDALUCÍA

WITH URSULA A. FEILER:
NOCH MEHR ANDALUSISCHE GESCHICHTEN

WITH DAVID LÓPEZ:
MÁS MISTERIOS ANDALUCES

CONTENTS

PREFACE

This is not a history book, it is more a romantic imagining of the story of a village, its history, people and culture, set in a historical framework.

In its totality, the book is *la historia del pueblo,* the story of a village. In Spanish the word *'pueblo'* means village, it also has the meaning of the people, especially the common people. The word *'historia'* also has a double meaning, that of story certainly, but also of history. And so it is with this book, which is the story of both the village and its inhabitants through time.

The early settlers of the region in the Neolithic age were almost certainly from the eastern Mediterranean area, who settled locally around Almería and Antequera. These early settlers were followed in turn by the Phoenicians, who developed trade, and named the land 'i-shephan-im' (meaning full of rabbits), and then in their turn by the Greeks. The Greeks were responsible for the further development of trade and the exploitation of local resources. They are said to have been the first to export products such as esparto grass, from which the rope bridge across the Dardanelles (the Hellespont) is thought to have been constructed by Xerxes during the Greek war with Persia. They also extended the production of, and the export of, the local mineral deposits, and developed the cultivation of both grapes and olives.

The Greeks were then followed by the Romans, who also did much to improve the area economically. As they did with most of Europe, the Romans brought order, organisation and the construction of roads, bridges and irrigation systems. They also brought the name Hispania to the country.

Each successive wave of invaders brought with them their own cultural influences, which in turn left a legacy. It was however the establishment of the Moorish rule that lasted, in this part of Spain, for over seven centuries that changed the culture most dramatically. The influence of that change can still be observed today. In 'Andalucía' even the name itself is derived from the Moorish title of al-Andalus.

The Moors established a thriving silk industry in this area, the pueblo becoming an important town. It, together with Canillas de Aceituno, became the centre of this trade. Several surviving large *mora,* mulberry, trees on which the silk worms lived can still be seen around the village. The very word Canillas comes from the manufacture of silk, and some people believe that the name Sedella does too. The locals, however, claim the name is derived from the battle that took place locally, when the Moors were driven from the village.

The village is one of the *pueblos blancos,* white villages, of the Axarquía, a hilly region that lies between Málaga to the west and Nerja to the east, and between the Mediterranean and the sierras inland.

The first chapter is an account of the village as it was when we first arrived in1994, and the last one of how it is now 22 years later. The remaining chapters trace the pueblo's history.

There are no written facts about the village in pre or early history, but there is general knowledge as to events in the area in which it is situated. In the early chapters, I have built a web of stories around this knowledge, and created characters and situations to fill them.

As the book progresses, then more is known about the village and its inhabitants. Such facts include amongst them the journey of one of the villagers to South America as a missionary; the murder of an ex-judge by the local mayor; the battle between the forces of Napoleon and the local guerrillas; the short stay in the village by Gerald Brennan, and the other events that can be found in the middle chapters. I have still fictionalised these chapters and invented characters to fill them.

Then there is the story of how the village got its name, a myth cherished by the people of the pueblo and which is recorded on the village shield. It may very well be true.

Much of the content of most of the later chapters concern tales told to me directly by people of the village, but in all but a few cases I have not used their real names.

The final three, before the last one about the village as it is today, are stories about the three fiestas I went to during my first year here.

Each of the historical chapters is in two parts. The first part is a fairly factual account of the relevant time, though some of these facts may be slightly altered in time etc. to fit the story. The second part of the chapter is a story set around these historical events.

None of the fictional characters in these stories bear any relationship with actual people, living or dead. Any factual errors are entirely my fault, for which I apologise. Where I may have changed the sequence of any events to fit the storyline, I plead 'artistic license'.

ACKNOWLEDGEMENTS

First of all, I must acknowledge the people of the *pueblo* of Sedella, without whose existence this book would not of course have been possible. They have been friendly and welcoming to Wendy and me since we first arrived, and many of the chapters owe much to comments made to us and stories told by them to us.

My thanks also go to Andy and Mags. This book is based on one I wrote years ago, with quite a bit of reordering, omissions and additions. A & M read that first book for me and helped edit it into its final form. Even though it was not published at the time, their effort then has now flowered in this book. One argument we had was over the phrase 'the Catholic Kings', which is a direct translation from the Spanish *Los Reyes Católicos.* They wanted me to put 'the Spanish King and Queen', as we would in England. However, these two rulers were monarchs in their own right, Isabella of Castile and Ferdinand II of Aragon. Their marriage brought together the two thrones and helped to make Spain one country, and this is why they are called here in Spain *Los Reyes Católicos.* That is one argument they didn't win, but my thanks go to them for their work on the original script.

As always, I have to acknowledge the assistance given in editing, typing and formatting this book for Amazon by Wendy. Without her, this story would never have seen the light of day.

John Hardy, Sedella 2016

CHAPTER 1

SEDELLA 1994 - THE PUEBLO AS IT WAS WHEN I FIRST ARRIVED

The *pueblo*, village, where I live is one of the *pueblos blancos*, white villages, of Andalucía. A Spanish hill town, in which many of its buildings reflect the historic Moorish influence of the *'Mudéjar'* style. The village is about 700 metres above sea level on the slopes of the Sierra Tejeda below the high summit of La Maroma, which at 2069 metres is the highest peak in the province of Málaga.

The sierra falls steeply from the high peaks and ridges overlooking the village, down to the level of the pueblo itself. From here, the land runs down to the coastal plain below in a series of interlacing fingers or ridges. These ridges have steep rocky sides down to small streams, which meander through them and finally join together to eventually discharge into the Mediterranean Sea.

The pueblo stands about 15 km inland as the crow flies (if there were any crows locally), but some 30 km by road from the coast. This road runs to and from the coast in a large arc, with the pueblo roughly at its apex.

To the west of the village, the nearest town is Canillas de Aceituno about 8 km away, whilst to the east the nearest, even smaller, pueblo is Salares, which is some 4 km distant.

The road from Canillas was only extended to the pueblo in the early 1960's, and that to Salares constructed shortly after. This road then terminated at Salares; from here the road to Árchez, the next town, was unsurfaced. Prior to the road link to Canillas, all transport into and out of the village was by mule track. A local historian, Manuel Fernández Mota, relates how, when a young man, he was journeying to the pueblo from Salares, and asked a local farmer how far the two villages were from each other. *"Un cigarro de camino,"* was the answer, in other words a cigarette away. Manuel Fernández recalls how he found the answer a trifle romantic, but on the other hand accurate. He lit a small cigar on leaving Salares, and finished it on

9

reaching the village by way of goat and mule tracks. This was of course before the road existed.

The village is built in an 'h' shape, on two *lomos* or ridges, running roughly east to west with a cup shaped valley between the two feet of the 'h'. The road from Canillas to Salares runs to the south of the village and connects with the top of the upright and both feet of the 'h', giving three entrances for traffic but with no viable through road. The streets and alleys inside the village are crooked and narrow, with only a few being wide enough to allow a single car to drive through. These narrow streets were originally used only for the passage of horses or mules. Where the streets run down the sides of the ridges, they are stepped at irregular intervals with drops of varying heights. Most of the *calles,* streets, are surfaced, if only roughly, with only a few still unsurfaced.

A small hill overlooks the village, at the pivot of the 'h', on which are the ruins of a Moorish fort. From here, you can look down over the whole pueblo spread out below, and also follow the line of the road on both sides of the village. The strategic importance of the fort, both in dominating the villagers and defending it from attack, needs little imagination.

As one approaches the village from the west, by way of Canillas de Aceituno, the first sight is of Casa Pinta, a newly built bar, restaurant and hostal, lying to the left hand side of the road. The hostal derives its name from the house that once stood on the site and was owned by Rafa Redondo, who apparently always had it painted in a variety of colours, hence the name 'paint house'. Rafa sold the house to his friend, Francisco Conde Gálvez, who built the new hostal. Francisco, or Paco in one of its diminutive forms, and his wife Carmen, though both from the village, now live in Málaga, where he drives a taxi. Because of this, he rents out the hostal. When we were looking at property to buy, two years prior to moving here, Casa Pinta was not yet built.

It was at Casa Pinta that, shortly after our arrival in the village, we were in the bar having a drink with Rafa Redondo who we knew well, and from whom we had bought one of our mules. At that time, Paco had no one renting the bar and was therefore having to manage it himself, with the help of various part-time staff. That particular night he was on his own and, as well as serving at the bar, was cooking in the kitchen and serving in the restaurant. There were two groups in the restaurant, one couple well on with their meal but causing problems by sending their main course back for being too cold, and another group of four English holiday makers, who were renting a house in the village. Paco had a menu but it was only in Spanish, and so Wendy, my wife, went into the restaurant to help translate it for them. Whilst she was there with them Rafa Redondo, who had gone into the kitchen to talk to Paco, came out and told me that Paco had *muchos problemas,* many problems. He simply could not manage on his own to run the bar and the restaurant at the same time. When Wendy returned to the bar, she could not find me. I was in the kitchen, together with Rafa, helping Paco prepare the meals. That night, for us, all the drinks were on the house.

Continuing past Casa Pinta, the road turns a left hand bend and the village itself comes into sight. Immediately on the right at this point is a large open plan concrete area, this is the *recinto ferial,* fiesta site, on which the summer feria is held. Immediately above and to the rear of this is the football pitch. To the left of the road opposite the recinto is the open-sided summer bar, Bar Oasis, owned and run by Rafa, who also owns and runs Bar Chiringuito in the village itself. Rafa is confined to a wheelchair, the result of an accident when his car went over the edge of one of the ravines which are a feature of the road up to the village.

Further on is the main entrance to the village at the head of the 'h'. Here the road forks, one branch goes up a gentle slope into the *pueblo* whilst the main road continues downhill on to the south. On the right on the main road there are two large and fairly recently built bars. The first, directly opposite the road into the village, is Bar Andaluz, and the second is Bar Granada, about a couple of hundred metres further on.

Where it enters the village, the branch road only has buildings on the left. The first one is the house of Pepe Sánchez, who plays the cymbals in the town band and who, on Fridays, allows a bank, 'Unicaja', to use one of his rooms as a branch office. Just beyond Pepe's is a small tree-lined square in which is the doctor's surgery, the *farmacia,* chemists, the town washhouse with the old pensioners' club above, and the main village *fuente,* fountain, which has four continually running water points.

This square, on warm sunny days (therefore for most of the year) is the meeting place of the older men of the village, who sit lazily in the sun. There are plenty of walls for them to shelter behind out of the wind in the winter, whilst the trees give shade from the hot summer sun. Here they sit and argue endlessly over matters of little or no importance, but to which they hold fervently. I always say that if two Spaniards are discussing a matter, there will be three passionately held views.

Opposite the washhouse, on the right of the road, is the olive mill. The building is built on the side of the slope. The floor at road level is where the olives are taken to be weighed. They are then emptied into a hopper and dropped down to the lower level to be pressed. The mill is an old one and the olives are pressed between two large stones. This lower level opens above the main road, which has gone downhill after splitting from the village street, allowing what is left of the olives after several pressings to be dropped down directly into lorries below. This is a process which produces good quality cold-pressed olive oil, and uses gravity for the movement of the berries.

Beyond the square, there are houses on both sides of the street, including on the left Bar Chiringuito and Bar Lorena, and on the right the post office, home of Josefina, the local postmistress. The *calle,* street, then narrows and after a few metres splits in two, and then runs on both sides of the valley which is between the feet of the 'h'. The one to the south ends in the main square of the village.

This small square is usually quiet and sleepy in the heat of the day, but can come spectacularly alive in the evenings and at fiestas. Here are two more bars, Bar Plaza and Bar *Poquito Más*, a little more. In the corner of the square opposite Bar Plaza is an oldish house. It is thought that at one time this house belonged to the 'first lord of the town'. On it is a square tower, the *omenaje* tower, which is built in the *Mudéjar* style, each side of it having two arches with central columns. I have been told that in the Civil War, the Nationalist troops of Franco hung people from it.

At the east side of the square stands the church of San Andrés, which is raised above the level of the square, and is reached by a wide flight of steps which give access to an open area at its front. Immediately to the right of the steps, on a level with the square, is the small village indoor market which has a general store, a bread shop and a fishmonger.

The village church and the *salon,* parish rooms, to its right are of fairly recent origin, having been reconstructed in the 1960's. The original church was much larger and took up all the space occupied by the present one, the *salon* and the open space in front of them both. This church, especially the tower, was initially structurally damaged by the earthquake of 1884, and then further damaged in the Civil War. The old church was a fine building in the Moorish style, said to resemble in many ways the one at Canillas de Aceituno, whilst the modern one, though adequate for its purpose and not unpleasing from the front, does not have the same architectural merit of its predecessor.

Inside the church there are statues of the Virgin, San Anton (the village saint) and a large dramatic crucifix. The last two are carved out of wood and are the work of Pepe Bravo, a self-taught local sculptor. They are his gift to the parish.

On the far side of the church is another square, in which there is a small supermarket, and from which the road then runs past the cemetery and rejoins the main road as it passes to the south of the village.

Going back to the point where the streets split to run either side of the valley, the one to the north passes a small general store, and a house which is said to be the one in which Gerald Brennan stayed on his journey from Granada to Málaga. He describes, in 'South from Granada', how he reached the town when darkness had fallen after scrambling down the sharp knife-edged ridges and screes on the slopes of the Sierra Tejeda. He arrived very late at last in Sedella, covered in sweat and scratches. He found that the good *posada* he had been recommended to stay in was no longer there, and so he had to take lodgings with an old crone, who gave him a supper of eggs fried in rancid fat, and provided a bed full of bugs. Brennan was probably the first English visitor to Sedella, not the small patrol of sailors that I envisage in the tale of the village at the time of the Peninsular War. You will look in vain for a red-headed descendant of these sailors, however there is in another pueblo, not many miles to the west of here, two red-headed brothers, who definitely show both by their colouring and facial structure such probable ancestry.

Just past Brennan's *posada* to the left of the street is the *ayuntamiento,* town hall, and then, where the road bends to the right to run down the north side of the valley, is the building that used to be the quarters of the Guardia Civil when they maintained a small force in the pueblo. This is now a private dwelling, a large house built around a central courtyard, overlooked by balconies, and in which there is a continually running fountain. This courtyard can only be viewed from the road if two pairs of large doors are open, one pair opening on to the street and the other at the end of a passage on to the courtyard itself.

The road then runs down to the school and the house of the *guardia forestal*, country park ranger, and then on past the *Ermita de Esperanza,* raised above the road level. Nearby is a small hill with an open space, where a Calvary is raised at Eastertide.

The road then continues to join the main Canillas to Salares road as it passes to the south of the pueblo.

Between the two ridges, between the legs of the 'h', the houses are built down both sides of the valley, whilst the very bottom is occupied by an avocado plantation, a vegetable garden and to the east of them a goat shed.

In Sedella there are about 515 adults plus the children. Many of the population either work outside the village in nearby towns, such as Vélez-Málaga, Nerja, Torre del Mar and Málaga, or are unemployed. The only occupations in the village are the public officials, such as postmistress, forest rangers, village policeman, schoolteacher and town hall staff; and service providers such as shopkeepers, bar and restaurant owners and staff, the bus driver and the builders. Any other local employment is to be found in the *campo,* where the principal occupations are goat-keeping, there being at least five sizable herds plus a few smaller ones, producing milk and meat;

and cultivating crops such as vines, grown to make raisins and local wine; olives, which are pressed into oil in the local mill belonging to the village cooperative; and almonds, which are sold to processors in Vélez-Málaga.

Most of the goats are housed inside the village and are taken out to graze in the surrounding *campo,* countryside. Because both goats and mules live in the village itself, they are often seen passing through the *calles*. This, of course, means that their droppings are to be seen everywhere, making work for the unemployed doing their *quincena* sweeping the streets. The *quincena* is a fifteen day work stint that unemployed people do from time to time. Whilst doing this, they earn slightly more than their unemployment pay. The people on their *quincena* are used by the *ayuntamiento*, town hall, for cleaning the streets, painting public buildings, building works and much more besides.

All round the village there are *bancales,* small irrigated and cultivated plots on terraces, on which are grown vegetables for home consumption, maize and barley for animal fodder, and fruit such as oranges and lemons. There are also fig, pomegranate, the occasional *mora,* mulberry, and carob trees scattered around the *campo*. The moras are reminders of the silk industry that was once important in the area, whilst the carobs are mainly used for animal fodder. The figs, which are largely now not harvested, were once an important food source. During the years following the Civil War, when food was scarce, there are stories of *campesinos,* peasants, whose only breakfast whilst working on the land was a handful of dried figs.

Because of the nature of the *campo,* which consists of steep-sided ridges and valleys where tractors cannot be used, the village has many mules which are used for ploughing and transporting the local crops. These mules are stabled in the lowest floor of the village houses, often together with a few chickens. Because the village is built on the sides of hills, these stables usually open out onto side streets with the house itself opening onto the main street above.

Given the shortage of local employment and the hard nature of the work in the *campo,* a large number of the young men leave the village to work elsewhere for a period of years, returning eventually

15

with their savings. This exodus from the village takes the emigrants to such places as Sevilla, Barcelona, Madrid and so on in Spain, but perhaps strangely often to other European countries, mainly Switzerland. Such emigration is not a recent phenomenon but has been going on for many years, since, in fact, well before the Civil War.

The isolated nature of the pueblo, together with its harsh way of life, has resulted in a population that is sturdily independent, with a complicated web of family ties that permeate the village, so that everyone seems to be a *primo,* cousin of everyone else.

This then is *mi pueblo,* my village, which has all the traditional contradictions and passionate splendours of the region. A village of narrow, crooked, steep streets, blindingly white in the harsh sunlight with many shady corners. Everywhere red geraniums give splashes of colour against the harsh white cal-coated walls. The village is set, like an iced cake, mid the grey violet hard rocks of the sierras, tempered by the pink and white almond blossom in January.

Quiet, sleepy and welcoming, the town can burst into sound, light and wild extravagance at the drop of a fiesta.

CHAPTER 2

TODO COMENZÓ
(It all began)

Nothing is known of course about the pueblo during the Bronze Age, indeed there may not have even been a settlement here at all. This book, however, is a romance and not a factual history. And given its location between two small rivers and the existence of a small hillock, easily defended, it is likely that one would have been established here. What is known about the area as a whole is that it was inhabited in the Bronze Age by a movement of people from North Africa. These people came from Egypt along the African shoreline, and crossed into Iberia near present day Almuñecar. From here they spread west along the coast, and then moved inland and established a settlement beyond the sierras at where Antequera now stands. Many remains of these two early settlements are still there to this day. From these two areas, on the coastal plain and on the hinterland beyond, they gradually also occupied the slopes of the sierras in between. There are conflicting views as to the origin of these early peoples. This first chapter gives two differing accounts of this history as given to the young people of the pueblo. The first is a poetic tale based on myth, and the second is a scientific one revolving around known archaeological facts and assumptions.

◊   ◊   ◊   ◊   ◊

The old man, the storyteller, gathered his small group of young listeners around him on the hillside overlooking the pueblo. He combed his fingers through his long grey beard, gathered it in his left hand and tugged it in his characteristic way. Smiling, he looked round the group, cleared his throat and started to speak.

"*Todo comenzó,* it all began ...." He paused then resumed. "Where did it begin? Where does anything begin? You could, perhaps, say it all began on the sixth day, when God created all living things, including man. Perhaps you could argue that it started with the great

17

flood that covered the earth. You could say that the beginning was when the first group of men reached this place."

The old man paused for a few moments, with his eyes closed, yet looking far beyond the horizon to things more distant in space and time. He stroked his beard again and, gathering it once more into his left hand, continued.

"It all began, in my story, one day on the boat. Ham, the second son, was angry. He was often angry. He thought that Shem, the first born, was his father's favourite, given pride of place in all things. Today, for instance, he was on deck in the open air, feeding the large animals that were housed there. There was no room for the elephants and camels in the holds of the ship. And Japheth, the youngest of the three of them, well, Ham thought that he was spoilt, given an easy life. He was tending the birds in their cages and the small furry animals, such as the rabbits and mice. Easy work. But Ham, here he was in the deep smelly hold, cleaning out the shit from the goats and the donkeys!

"Ham liked the bulls best, especially the black ones. He also liked the black pigs. His father looked after them though, whilst 'I get the stubborn donkeys and the silly old goats,' he muttered furiously to himself as he worked. 'When we land, when this flood goes down, if it ever does,' he continued, muttering as he forked up the litter, 'when it does, forty seven days now though and still no sign of it.'

"His muttering stopped short as he heard the raucous call of the raven flying overhead. His father had released it from its cage seven days ago, trying to find out if the bird could spot any dry land. Since then the creature had been circling the ship, crying out mournfully all the time. At least it would irritate Shem up there on the deck, he thought maliciously. Today his father was going to let a dove loose, to see if that could find dry land. 'When we do find land,' he continued his muttering, 'then I'll take my wife and my concubines, my children, slaves, animals; the lot, all my share and go off. We'll go somewhere warm and sunny, by the sea, cut off from all the rest of them by mountains. Somewhere different.'

"As he worked and muttered, he brought himself out of his bad temper, as he always did. He laughed at himself, he was a pleasant young man, of a naturally sunny disposition. But one minute he was up, the next down. Sun and shade, dry and wet, hot and cold. Just like you, Ramon," the old man said, fixing his twinkling eyes on the youngster.

Ramon was a peasant, sturdily built, young and fierce in his views. He squirmed under the gaze of the storyteller, whilst his companions laughed, enjoying his embarrassment.

"But, like you, strong, a good worker and, when you're not getting hot under the collar, pleasant company and a generous friend." The rest of the group nodded agreement to this assessment of Ramon's character.

"Ay, ay, ay," the old man continued, beard pulling all the time. "Ham did just that, he took all his tribe, who we call the Hammites, out of Egypt and along the coast of North Africa, just over the sea .... there."

Here he paused again and pointed. Over the slopes of the hills at their feet, over the blue sea. Beyond the sparkle of the sun reflected off the water, to the blue haze of the distant coastline. Morocco, home of the Moors.

"Ay, ay, ay .... it took years, of course, centuries, long after the death of Ham, and of his sons: Cush, Mizraim, Put and Canaan. Of their sons too - Sheba, Nimrod, the mighty hunter, and all the rest of them.

"In the end they reached that distant shore. They crossed the sea and landed near what we now call Almuñecar and settled down. This was the land dreamed of by Ham in the dark smelly hold of the ark. A dream passed down from generation to generation on the long journey. Somewhere warm and sunny, fertile, near the sea and cut off by mountains from the rest of the world. Somewhere different. Here they also found minerals, copper and tin, from which they made bronze. With the bronze they made weapons, swords, shields and spearheads; and tools, hoes and ploughs. They also made jewellery..... like this brooch." The old man took out an intricate piece of jewellery that he had found years ago, a relic of that distant past. He passed it round the group and, whilst they were admiring it, used the pause to drink deeply from the wine by his side. Settled again, the group waited for him to finish his refreshment, groom his beard, clear his throat and begin again.

"Ay, ay, ay, so they had fish from the sea, grain, vegetables, nuts and berries from the land, and plenty of game to hunt. And of course they had bulls, black bulls, and black pigs too. Just like our famous black Iberian pigs of today. But they also had the goats and the donkeys. Oh yes! Goats for milk, cheese and meat, and donkeys for work, Ham's descendants couldn't get away from the goats and the donkeys. Just like you, Pedro, you keep goats and a donkey ...... well, yes, I know it's a mule, but its father was a donkey. Old Antonio's donkey, wasn't it?" The old man chuckled and continued. "Over time they spread east and west, up and down the coast. Some came to Málaga, just down there," he pointed again. "Then they moved inland to Menga, what we call Antequera, just over the mountain. Some of you have been to the chambers they built there. How they moved those large stone Megaliths .... it's beyond belief.

"Some people say that these same builders, or their descendants, went to England about a thousand years later. To a place called Stonehenge, to help the English build their famous circle of stones.

"Ay, ay, ay, whatever the truth of that, the chamber at Menga, as some of you have seen, has thirty large stones, each weighing 130,000 kilos they say. What effort, what labour! With only a few donkeys." He rocked with laughter. "At Antequera, of course, they had the *vega*. The fertile plain, where they could grow crops. And raise their beloved bulls! Soon they were spreading along the Guadalquivir River. Agriculture improved, more copper........ and silver too was found in the Sierra Morena.

"Ay, ay, ay, centuries of development .....

"But what has this to do with the pueblo, you say? What have we to do with Almuñecar, Antequera or even Málaga, let alone the Sierra Morena or the river Guadalquivir?"

The old man paused again and gazed at the pueblo near to where they were sitting. It was perched part way down the slope of the Sierra Tejeda, above the town of Vélez-Málaga, which was out of sight below near the coast, and he smiled. Once more he stroked his beard, then gathered it up, into his left hand, as if also gathering his thoughts, and took up the story again.

"Ay, well," he sighed. "One of Ham's descendants, a straight line of descent no doubt, certainly of a like temperament; a chip off the old block. Let's call him Hamito, little Ham. Well, Hamito, like Ham before him, was dissatisfied. Not for him a life of a fisherman on the coast, or a miner of copper nor yet a farmer on the *vega*. Not for him a life tending his father's goats and donkeys. No! He wanted to explore, and hunt and discover new places. His father, like Ham's father before him, kept him busy with the family goats and donkeys. So, one day, he decided to leave his home near Antequera, leave the easy life of the fertile plain, and go off with his wife and concubines and children and slaves.....

"He came over the pass at Zafarraya and along the slopes of the mountain. He searched for weeks until he found a small hilltop with two rivers nearby for water. That hilltop over there, where the ruins of the old Moorish fort are." The old man pointed once more, his thin arm straight out in front of him. "Here they settled. They exchanged the easily worked land of the *vega* for these steep slopes; the flat plain for the deep valleys; the lush grassland for rocky soil and sharp prickly undergrowth. But there was game to hunt, plenty of it; berries and nuts; trees to fell to make houses; stones to build walls and make more permanent homes. They levelled some areas to grow corn and vegetables. And they brought with them their beloved bulls, black bulls, and the black Iberian pigs. They also brought their goats and donkeys though! Hamito, like Ham before him, couldn't get away from his goats and donkeys. Just as we can't. Bulls may be romantic, dramatic even. Some of you, I know, relish the bull fights in the ring at Málaga..... no, not you, Jorge, I know, you prefer the football stadium to the bullring. And the black pigs may give the best Serrano ham; but we need, as did Ham and Hamito, the goat and the donkey. The goat for milk and cheese.... yes, yes and *chivo*, goat's meat, as well. And the donkey and mule to plough the land and carry our crops."

The old man paused for the last time. "Ay, ay, ay, that's where it all began, with Ham on the boat, mucking out his goats and donkeys. And here, in the pueblo, is where it ended...." he sighed. "Except, as

21

there is no one beginning, so there is also no true end. It will go on and, one day, one of you will be telling the story, not me. And adding to it too...... and so on and on until the last day, when God will collect in all his creatures and pull down the curtain. And now, I want my dinner, so off you all go."

The old man rose from his seat, his young audience rising with him and, laughing and shouting, made their way back to the pueblo.

That's one explanation but there is another.

The professor, a small neat, brisk man of about forty, black-haired with a handsome moustache, wearing metal-framed spectacles, entered the lecture room at Málaga University. He was the professor of history, and also of archaeology. The day was hot and the students drowsy. It was the final lecture of Friday, and already thoughts of the coming weekend were forming in the students' heads.

The professor's subject today was the Bronze Age in Andalucía.

"In about 3000 BC," he began in a firm authoritative voice, "in the Danube valley, or possibly in Egypt, a movement of people began which spread along the North African coast. There are two schools of thought as to the origin of these peoples. One is that they were the Hammites, so called as they were believed to be descendants of Ham, one of the sons of Noah. The other, which I believe to be more likely, is that they were refugees fleeing before the rapidly developing deserts of North Africa. Whatever their roots, or route," he paused, and waited for the students to give a half-hearted laugh at his pun, then went on. "Whatever their roots, they reached Almuñecar by about 2500 BC, having crossed the Mediterranean Sea. Here they formed the culture that we know as 'the culture of Los Millares'. The ruins of the capital of this culture can still be seen near Almuñecar today. Indeed, I have worked there myself on some of the ruins.

"It is from here that the so called 'era of the megaliths' is said to emanate - the dolmens that are found all over Europe today. The development of the civilization centred around Almuñecar owed its success, and expansion, to the nearby mineral deposits, tin, copper and the like. The mining of these minerals led, of course, to the production and exploitation of bronze, for use as both tools and weaponry. Hence the name 'the Bronze Age'."

The professor noticed that some in the class were beginning to doze off. The late afternoon sun and his dry tone were combining to form a soporific mix. He raised his voice and battled on.

"Later, they spread up and down the coast, fishing being one of their main sources of food. They were, of course, hunter gatherers but were rapidly developing agricultural methods, aided by their use of metal tools."

Felipe was day dreaming. Gazing out of the window, lulled into a semi-hypnotic state by the drone of the professor's voice, the heat and thoughts about the coming weekend. Tonight, when he got off the bus in the pueblo at 8.30 pm, he would call in at Bar Plaza on his way home. Here he would have a coke and meet some of his friends who, unlike him, did not travel to Málaga every week to attend the university, but lived in the village all the time.

.... "This was the great age of architecture..... The megalith dolmens around Antequera, just to the north of Málaga........ The Menga chamber is composed of some thirty...... " The professor's voice drifted in and out of his consciousness. On Saturday, tomorrow, he would go up to the football pitch perhaps, if his father didn't want him to go out with the goats, or prune the olives....... his father would though, there was always work to be done. However, on Sunday evening, he would go up to Casa Pinta. All the crowd would be there, all his mates, and all the girls. He'd see some of them on Saturday evening as well, at band practice in the *salon*.

"By 2000 BC, the Millares culture of Almuñecar was drawing to a close." The professor stopped talking. No one was listening. He looked round and chose one of them at random. "Felipe," he snapped. "What date did the culture of Millares begin to decline?"

The class came awake, aware of the change of mood, the sudden challenge. All but one gave sighs of relief.

"Why me?" thought Felipe. "Why does he always get at me?" He searched in his subconscious for the answer, reaching for the half-heard words. "Er... about.... er .... about 2000 BC," he managed at last, not sure if he'd got it right.

"Good," said the professor in surprise, he was sure Felipe had not been paying attention. "Now ....."

"Señor," interrupted Felipe. "What about the ruins at, er, at Antequera, have you been on digs there?" That will keep him busy, he thought. He likes nothing better than to talk about his main hobby, archaeology.

"Yes, well yes, I have indeed. Last year I went......" The professor was now launched happily on to his favourite topic and this would see the day out. Felipe sank gratefully back into his soporific state. These Hammites, or whoever they were, probably came to my pueblo, he thought. They were perhaps the first inhabitants, my forefathers. I wonder what they looked like, how they lived, what they did. Did they have goats like my father? Did they have mules like ours?

Soon the end of the lesson came, the end of the college day, the end of the week for the students too. The professor and all the class left the room and the college. Felipe caught the bus which took him to Sedella, to keep his date with the Bar Plaza.

Two accounts of how it all began. Choose which you will! Myth or reality; folk lore or fact; romance or reason; poetry or science. Whichever you choose, neither is true. For things done can never be truly recalled. Ask any policeman investigating an accident seen by several onlookers, they will all have their own version. All of them correct but all of them different. Or get three people to describe a person they all know - there will be three different descriptions, similar perhaps but different.

With things that happened five or six thousand years ago, who can tell? Who fully knows the truth? The old storyteller, who talks of feelings and motives, and tales passed down over generations? Or the professor who uses excavations, old documents and scientific processes?

Why not choose both and blend them together? Why not visit the pueblo, or any other pueblo, and see the sights, listen to the people. They all carry genes dating back into the past. Genes mixed and honed and refined by what follows. Something of those far off days remains underneath all the future, which is now also the past.

This too is the purpose of this book, to put a romantic picture of the pueblo into a historic framework.

"Todo comenzó, it all began..........."

CHAPTER 3

PAX ROMANA
(The Roman Peace)

For several centuries after the decline of the Millares culture, very little changed in the small hill villages of the Axarquía. On the nearby coast, however, things were very different. Successive waves of Greeks and Phoenicians established a hold there, and spread north into the fertile plains and valleys. They developed ports in the towns of Gades (Cádiz), Malaca (Málaga) and Sexi (Almuñecar) close to the region. At the same time, hordes of Celts pressed southwards from the north, bringing with them iron tools and weaponry, and merging with the local Iberians to create a new race, the 'Celtiberians'.

Gades became the main trading port of the area, where all these and many other races merged. Sited ideally at the meeting point of the Atlantic and Mediterranean seas, it was a focal point for trade.

These differing cultures brought with them an era of strife and unrest, as well as much cultural and economic development. The Greeks were responsible for the development of both the vine and the olive for the production of wine and olive oil, and also the exploitation of esparto grass in the manufacture of rope and basketry work. The Phoenicians developed the local mining and fishing industries, bringing in return an influx of many artefacts such as alabaster goods and cosmetics. They were also responsible for the establishment of a written Iberian language.

Despite this turmoil on the coast and further inland, not much changed in the pueblo that is central to this story. Some benefit was obtained from the use of iron tools in farming; the improvements in the vines and olive trees gave an increase in their yields and a chance to trade in their products; the local esparto grass became a cash crop for export as both a raw material and also as goods fabricated in the village. Brought inland from the coast, salt and salted fish became available in larger quantities as a result of an increase in the trading of local products. But little else of the new civilizations washed up the hillside.

A number of the younger local men left the village to fight for the various groups competing for ascendancy in the region. These tough, fierce hill men were valued as warriors and received a good return for their services as mercenaries. Those who eventually returned to the pueblo brought with them not only comparative wealth, but also women from one of the various races struggling for supremacy in the peninsula.

The order that was eventually brought to the country by the Punic influence from Carthage also did little to affect the traditional life of the villages in the inhospitable hills, except reduce the exodus of fighting men and increase the volume of trade. The villagers of the locality carried on much as before, with the more adventurous travelling down to the coast or over the hill, to sell or barter the local produce rather than join in the fighting. These mercenary and trading ventures, together with the arrival in the village of refugees fleeing the periods of tumult on the coast, introduced sufficient new blood into the restricted local gene pool to ensure a healthy populace.

The Roman invasion of Gades in 218 BC, whilst the Punic leader Hannibal was crossing the Alps with his elephants and army to challenge Rome itself, was at first of no importance to the pueblo. The defeat of Hannibal and the establishment of a regional capital at Italica (Sevilla) by the Romans were likewise barely known of in the wild sierras. Slowly, the Romans extended their hold and control of the whole of Iberia, and by the turn of the century the legions were marching up and down the coastline below the village on the famous new road, the Via Herculia, now the route of the N340. The Via Herculia was constructed along the entire shore of the Mediterranean from Galia (France) in the north to Gades in the south. This road, first built and established by Rome, has never since ceased to be important in the history of Iberia, and is today well known and travelled, not by Roman legions or even the armies of Napoleon, but by hordes of tourists visiting the various Costas.

Even this activity below the village, and the new order and laws brought by the Romans, had little impact on the traditional life of the village. No legions ventured into the wild foothills of the Axarquía, and little Roman law or order was introduced into the individualistic lifestyle of the small villages of the region, the pueblo included.

The Romans introduced a new system of land ownership in Iberia that was to persist, in certain areas, almost until the present day. In the fertile areas and plains of the coastline and *vegas*, they granted large tracts of land to men of status and power, who often lived far away and never visited their property. The control of these lands was left to the *villicus,* bailiff, and led to the creation and growth of a new class of people, the landless labourer. This new system, the latifundia, was not extended into the *serrania,* mountain districts, which were considered too poor and remote to divide up in this way, leaving the smallholding peasantry still undisturbed. The latifundia were responsible for much of the agrarian unrest down the centuries, being finally one of the sparks that brought about both the rule of Primo de Rivera and later the Civil War in the 1930's. The establishment of landless labourers in the latifundia on the fertile lands, and the continuing presence of small peasant farmers in the *serrania*, explains the growth of the labour unions in the former and the rise of anarchism in the latter, both factors in the Civil War.

The position of the pueblo in the foothills of the *serrania* was another reason why Roman influence was slow in reaching it. The first effect Rome had in this area was in the increase of trade. The Roman consumption of vast quantities of both olive oil and wine increased the need for more production of both by the hill farmers. At the time, the new Roman settlements on the *vega,* on the other side of the mountain, brought a demand for salt, salt fish and fish paste, which led to an increase in traders passing through the area.

It was not until the arrival in the village, the pagus as he called it, of Gius Scipius in the early part of the first century BC, that the influence of Rome was finally felt, bringing with it the most major changes since its establishment. Gius was no centurion at the head of 100 men, simply the captain of a small party of soldiers, some thirty in number, part of a cohort stationed on the coast. He was to be, however, the official Roman magistrate of the pagus by the authority of the regional governor seated in Italica.

His section arrived at the pagus on an afternoon in September when most of the villagers were absent in the *campo,* busy with the grape harvest and other tasks. They were watched with suspicion and some hostility by the few women, children and old people left behind, as they planted the Roman eagle on its standard in the centre of the small market square of the village.

Gius then read out a proclamation to the villagers. He was a Roman citizen from the north of Italy, and his language was unintelligible to the local inhabitants. He had however brought with him in his group an Iberian mercenary, who translated for their benefit. This proclamation gave control of the pagus, its people and all its future life into his, Gius', hands as representative of the Emperor in Rome. From this time, the laws of Rome would apply to all transactions and features of the village. One of the women quickly sent her young son out into the *campo* to find the village headman and bring him back at once. The small Roman contingent had left the coast by the normal trade route, passing through Valverdes and entering the village from the west. A few of the locals working in that area had observed their progress and already sent word to Algar, the headman. The boy was met by a small group with him at its head as it approached the pagus. These villagers, therefore, soon entered the square to confront the Roman contingent.

Gius eyed the locals with interest and some unease. Already the villagers outnumbered his own men and Gius knew that there were still more in the *campo* who had not yet had word of the new arrivals or who, for one reason or another, could not leave their work to return straight away. The men of the pagus were short, squat and black-haired, dressed in roughly woven tunics and carrying primitive tools, and as such were no different to the other Iberians he had already encountered since his arrival in the province of Hispania, a short time previously. He was aware, however, that they would have weapons in their homes within easy reach. He was likewise aware of the reputation such people had gained as fierce warriors over the past centuries.

A long and protracted discussion now followed between the two men through the medium of the translator. Algar was alternately supported and encouraged by, and then argued with and interrupted by his supporters amongst the villagers. It is ever thus in Iberia. At last, a compromise solution was reached. In the coming days, the Romans would build themselves a fort on the top of the small hill which overlooked the village, where a half-ruined fortification from long past still stood. They would use their slaves for this work, and pay the locals for any materials or labour they required from them. Gius also undertook to buy supplies of food and wine as necessary for the use of his men. In return, he offered the villagers the status of free peasantry in the Roman state, and recognition by Rome of the existing land holdings. Alger would also be given the right to sit with him to discuss all matters of law that arose, and would be allowed to continue as local headman under license from Rome.

The alternative to this, he implied, or to any display of force against his group, would be the arrival in the pagus of a much larger band of Roman soldiers. This larger force would subdue the village and take its inhabitants into slavery. Remote as they were, the locals were well aware of the might of Rome in Iberia, and the size and number of the local legions. They had, in fact, been dealing with the regime for many years in trade and had long expected such a visit.

Reluctantly, therefore, they agreed to his terms and so became, together with all the rest of the local area, under the rule of the *Paz Romana,* the Roman peace. They were in this no different to most of Europe where, at that time, the Pax Romana reigned supreme. What disturbed the villagers most was the presence of the Roman slaves who arrived to carry out the projects undertaken by Gius. They had heard of the existence of these, had indeed witnessed runaway slaves passing through the village. They even had two or three of them living there at the time, by now integrated into the village populace, whose presence they took care to keep from the newcomers. But to have actual slaves in the pagus was anathema to these fiercely independent and free-living peasants.

Another point of dispute between the new Roman overlords and the locals was that of religion. Gius soon tried to stamp out the forms of local worship that were centred on natural objects, such as the mountains, trees and animals, and revolved around yearly events like midsummer and midwinter. In place of these, which he considered pagan gods, he wanted to introduce the Roman ones of Jupiter, Hercules and the one he was most in favour of, Mithras.

When the Roman troops first arrived in the village, the houses were built of adobe and stone. They brought with them a new material, lime, which when mixed with the local earth turned the adobe that was used for jointing and rendering the dwellings into a more permanent cement. The new arrivals also improved the water supply, channelling the small local streams to use for both drinking and irrigation. They also constructed a small pond above the village to store water in the dry summer months.

Gius also organised the importation into the village of tiles produced by the new brickyards in the region of what is now Vélez-Málaga, where the prolific local brick earth was burnt in rough clamps.

Gius, like many others in the Roman army, was by profession an engineer. The main reason he had been sent to the pagus was to improve the route between the rapidly growing town of Vélez and the rich *vega* beyond the high hills of the sierra. It was impossible, due to the terrain, to build a wide Roman via such as the many that drew straight lines over much of Europe. Nevertheless, a path using similar techniques could be constructed to improve the winding mule tracks of the present route, which were at times often impassable.

His first task was to construct a stone arch bridge over the deep gorge of the river, *'el arroyo de la fuente'*, just to the north of the village. Such was the success of this that the same bridge can still be crossed today by anyone walking out of the village by this footpath. From this point, the Romans laid a stone-paved way, about a metre wide, which snaked its route up the hillside to finally cross the crest of the sierra to the east of the high peak of Maroma, close to the lower summit of Cuascuadra. Once over the ridge, the route then dropped down to the fertile plain below. Here Gius' road met that of another constructed by his contemporary, who had laid one from what is now Alhama de Granada to the foot of the hill.

Later, he built a second route from the village close by, Salares, which joined the first one shortly after crossing the ridge, the arch bridge at the beginning of this path is also still in existence today.

With the passage of the years, the pagus benefitted from the increase in trade that the improved means of communication brought with it. The towns steadily growing in the interior, both in size and number, brought with them a growing demand for salted fish and 'garum', the paste made on the coast from fish. The demand for olive oil and wine also increased from these expanding urban centres. All this, coupled with the increasing passage of goods through the area of crops and products such as ironware, grain and meat, brought about a constant flow of traders using the newly improved ways through the hills. To cope with the increasing volume of traffic, a small inn was built in the village, and another near the summit of the climb, to house the traders who plied to and fro across the hill.

In 38 BC, Hispania was officially absorbed into Rome and many of the previously conquered were granted full citizenship, some even being allowed into the elite. In time Hispania would even produce Roman emperors, the first Trajan followed by Hadrian, both being born in Italica. Locally, several inhabitants of the pagus were granted artisan status, amongst them the miller of wheat, the fabricator of esparto goods, and the miller and producer of oil from the local olives. Whilst there was still a small corps of soldiers garrisoned in the fort, all the village officials were once again drawn from the local inhabitants. The new village headman, or magistrate, holding his office under Imperial decree, was a descendant of the long dead Algar.

The Romans had brought with them law, order, improved communications, economic advance and, because of a gradual intermarriage, an improvement of the blood stock. *Paz Romana* was therefore, due mainly to its peaceful incursion into village life, of a beneficial nature.

38 BC also brought however another change into the whole of Hispania, the introduction of a general levy or tax. The levy, which

varied with the individual and depended upon such factors as land ownership, number of slaves held, volume of production of goods and such features of individual wealth, was nevertheless payable by all free peasants and artisans of the Empire. From this point, the nature of the village economy slowly changed, from one based on barter to one which evolved around cash. After an initial resistance to and resentment of this change, life in the pagus settled down into one that, despite all the changes, was not very different in nature to that which existed before the entry of Gius into the village.

CHAPTER 4

EN LOS PASOS DE SAN IAGO
(In the footsteps of St. James)

The Roman occupation of Spain brought many changes over time in communications, trade and law, and in many other matters, as it did to all of the countries where their writ prevailed.

In the *vega* above and on the coast below the village, the legions might still march; slaves suffer; landless labourers, little better than slaves, work in the latifundia; rich merchants abound in Gades; Roman theatre and gladiatorial contests fill the amphitheatres at Malaca, Sexi, Gades and Italica; but here in the foothills of the Axarquía, life continued virtually undisturbed. The area reverted to the annual cycle of agricultural sequences, waiting for the next event that would disturb and in the end lead to the destruction of Pax Romana itself.

This event started in another pagus, far from the Axarquía, a pagus situated in a small Jewish state also ruled by Rome, at the further end of the Mediterranean Sea, in Nazareth.

After this event, Christianity spread through the Roman Empire, at first resisted and persecuted by the state but later, after the conversion of the Emperor Constantine, with the state's permission. In time, missionaries spread to all corners of the empire, the small pagus being no exception.

◊   ◊   ◊   ◊   ◊

The old man, Septimus, sat on a low wall in the warm winter sun beside the village fountain, in the shelter of a carob tree out of the wind. The fount was installed many years ago by the first Romans to arrive in the small pagus, and was now the centre of much of the life of the village. All around him women came and went, filling earthen jars and leather bottles from the continuously running flow of water, stopping to gossip as they did so. As they passed, they all greeted him with warmth and kindness, due not so much to his venerable age of 80, but more to his position as the retired deacon of the local church.

33

Deacon, the old man insisted to himself, not this new word that was spreading from the mother church in Rome, 'priest'.

Rome was much on his mind this morning, for he had just received word from Malaca, (Málaga) of the consecration in Rome a few weeks ago of Urban. In this message had come more evidence of the changes now taking place, of the rapidly growing tendency of the Church to try to standardise its faith, rituals, organisation and practices. This new leader in Rome was, for example, no longer just a bishop but a Pope, whatever that meant. He agreed with much that was taking place, like the standardisation of texts and the stamping out of heresies, but what was the point of altering the long established names of church officials? He had also heard of a move to try and force all deacons, or 'priests', he muttered to himself, to remain unmarried and celibate. Smiling, he thought of his own wife and children, it was too late for this change to affect him anyway.

His thoughts of Rome made him reminisce on his childhood growing up there. It was now nearly sixty years since he had left his home to travel here, never to return to the place of his birth. He had seen his mother only once since then, when she had journeyed to her own place of birth, Malaca, with one of his brothers, and spent a few weeks here in the pagus with him. But that was over forty years ago, and he had never seen her or anyone else of his family since. News of the deaths of both her and his father had been sent to him by his brothers, but since then he had heard no more from any of them.

From where he was sitting he could see, far off below, the waters of the Mediterranean shining silver bright in the January sun, and his thoughts were taken back over the years, to the day when at 21 he had been in a small trading boat crossing that same stretch of sea, heading to Malaca a few leagues away to the west.

That January morning, in 172 AD, he had been standing in the bows as the sailing vessel bowled along before the prevailing levanter. He had been very excited, not just that morning, but during the whole voyage from Rome, and looking forward with anticipation and optimism to the tasks ahead.

His excitement stemmed from many sources. At 21, this was the first time he had been away from Rome on his own. He had been setting out on what he now realised, looking back, was not just an adventure but a life's mission. He was the fourth son of a Roman senator and had lived, up until then, a privileged life. In time, his eldest brother would follow his father into the senate, and all three of his older siblings were at that time in the legions. He however had had no taste for army life and, following his parents' conversion into the new Christian religion some years previously, he had come under the influence of Bishop Soter, the first Christian bishop of Rome. Under Soter, he had become enthusiastic to join the great mission of the Church, and at 20 had been ordained as a deacon. The Church at that time was spreading throughout the Empire and he had determined to go to Hispania, to Malaca, birthplace of his mother, to join in the task of carrying the message beyond the shores of the land and into the interior.

On its journey, the boat had passed near to the town of Tarraco (Tarragona), birthplace of Pontius Pilate who had condemned Jesus to death. His thoughts on Pilate were mixed, as a Roman he shared the view that he had been an able governor, and as a Christian he did not know if he blamed him for the death, or valued his contribution to the crucifixion, and therefore the subsequent resurrection, which had led to the rise of the new religion. With him on the boat he had carried two scrolls which told of the life of Jesus, one of which castigated Pilate; the other describing him as a 'tool' doing God's will. The old man sighed at that point in his musings; he still did not know the answer to that one even now.

Another reason for his excitement that morning long ago was that he knew that he was following *en los pasos de San Iago*, in the footsteps of St. James. Just over 130 years previously, in about 40 AD, St. James, one of Jesus' disciples known as Boanergas (son of thunder), and brother of John, another of the disciples, had sailed this very route. James however had not stopped at Malaca, but had instead gone through the Pillars of Hercules and up the western shore of Lusitania (Portugal) to Iria Flavia (Padron), on the wild north west corner of Hispania (now known as Galicia). A few short years later, his body had been conveyed once more from Rome by the same route, after his beheading by Herod Agrippa on his return to the city. He was

35

then buried on the top of a small hill a short distance from Iria Flavia (at what is now Santiago de Compostella). Despite his shorter journey, stopping well short of the Pillars of Hercules, Septimus had been highly pleased at the thought of travelling in the wake of such a famous predecessor, with the same purpose and of carrying on his mission to the Iberians of the province.

The old man shifted in his seat beside the fountain to ease his stiffening limbs, and smiled to see another figure coming to join him. The newcomer was of roughly the same age as himself and was carrying his lute, without which he was never seen.

Sitting down, the other man greeted him. "And how are you, 'father' Septimus, still saving the good people of the pagus?" he asked ironically.

The old deacon replied, "And you, Ulpius, you old heathen, is there still no hope for you?"

After more friendly banter, the two lapsed into companionable silence, each to his own thoughts. Ulpius, thought the old man, was another reason for the pleasure and excitement of that long ago voyage. Septimus, as the son of a Roman senator, had never before had a friend who was not a member of one of the best families in the city. Ulpius, however, had certainly not been in that category at all. He was a strolling musician and had made what living he could playing at feasts, in the streets and at the games in the amphitheatre. He had never known his parents and had been brought up, as far back as his memory went, by various vagabonds who had taught him to play and sing. He was leaving Rome and returning to his homeland of Hispania for reasons he would not divulge to Septimus, but almost certainly, in the Roman youth's opinion, shady ones.

On the boat, however, they had struck up a firm friendship, which was to stand the test of time, despite Ulpius' derision of all forms of religion, Christianity included. It was on the boat, where they had first met, that he had taken to calling Septimus 'father', because he held the office of deacon, a habit that had not changed over the years.

When they reached Malaca, the two youths had separated, Septimus going to the house of the local bishop, whilst Ulpius had disappeared into the noisy lanes of the town. Septimus thought back to those first days in Malaca. He had been stunned by the town, almost frightened by it. In contrast to the orderly streets of the part of Rome where he had grown up, and the control under which the Imperial Guard held the city, Malaca was a cauldron. There was little control here, the locals were tumultuous in their way of life, noisy, unrestrained and constantly in upheaval. The streets teemed with sailors, traders, animals, minstrels (amongst them somewhere presumably Ulpius) and beggars. At night, much wine was consumed and various activities abounded. There were the girls from Gades who gave dancing displays accompanied by much shouting, stamping of feet, hand clapping and the rattle of castanets. Their songs rang out through all this noise, loud, clear and vibrant, changing in speed and pitch constantly. (It was this form of dancing that would lead Cádiz, many centuries later, to claim to be the home of the flamenco). Near the temple of Mithras, Roman soldiers and locals fought the famed large fierce black bulls of the region, anointing themselves with the blood after a kill, in honour of the God, Mithras. (This Mithrasian practice is claimed to be the origin of bull fighting by many.) Added to this were the usual Roman events in the amphitheatre, such as gladiatorial contests. Malaca at times had seemed, to the young arrival in the city, to be in continual upheaval.

The young deacon had been kept in the city for two years, during which time he had begun to familiarise himself with the local language and customs. At this time, the bishop had also explained how he was introducing the Christian religion by using the existing Roman religions, and merging and adapting their practices into Christianity. Such festivals as the Mithrasian one at midwinter he had subsumed into the Christmas rituals, the vernal equinox of springtime he had absorbed into Eastertide, and so on. Above all, Septimus had been told that in the countryside, where he was to be sent, he would find many pre-Roman practices still being followed, and that he must try to amalgamate these into his ministry, rather than reject them. He must learn to honour and use such things as the gathering of crops, the time of ploughing and the blessing of the beasts of the field, by attaching them to special Christian services. During these two years the young Roman, who had had a good education in Rome, listened and learned from his superior. Nothing, however, from his early schooling, his life in Malaca, nor his bishop's teachings, prepared him for the people and way of life he was to find in the pagus to which he was finally sent.

He had travelled east out of Malaca early one February morning on the next stage of his mission, reaching the small town of Mainake (Vélez-Málaga) in the early afternoon. Here, he had stayed overnight in the home of the local deacon before, the next morning, taking the well trodden trade route into the sierras through the small mean hamlet of Valverdes, and then further up the track to reach at last the pagus which is central to all our accounts.

His arrival at the village had gone almost unnoticed that day, he reflected. He had journeyed with a small group of mules loaded with fish and other produce, and entered the pagus in mid afternoon. It had been a cloudy day with a cool breeze. Such weather, which could persist for days, and he now knew to occur from time to time in the area, was in stark contrast to the usual balmy nature of the climate.

"We may as well be serving on the great wall of Hadrian in the far north of Britannia," grumbled an old legionnaire who had travelled with the small party, as they neared their destination.

"At least there there are warm baths to go to," rejoined another soldier, who had also served on the wall which the Emperor Hadrian had built to keep out the wild Celts from the north some fifty years earlier.

Septimus had travelled to the pagus as the new Roman recorder, or scribe, to the local authorities. It would be his task to act as secretary to the local army captain who was in charge of the small force garrisoned in the village; to also act as scribe to the village headman or magistrate; and to keep, and update, the village records of births, deaths, marriages and land ownership rights. He held this post under the authority of the Emperor, Marcus Aurelius. His other task of converting the populace to Christianity he held under the authority of Bishop Soter in Rome. Ever since the early days of the Church, it had been the practice of all its officials to keep themselves by their own labour. Paul himself had been a tent maker and had pursued this trade in many places. Septimus, as the pampered son of

38

a Roman citizen, had no trade to support him save his education, and the bishop at Malaca had obtained the post of scribe for him on the return of the previous one to Rome.

Whilst the villagers had gathered round the small caravan as it entered the pagus, greeting the traders and beginning their bargaining for their goods, Septimus recalled how he had been simply ignored, until spotted by a soldier who had taken him to the local magistrate. He had then been shown the house that went with his position as scribe, and left to his own devices.

Thinking back now over the years, he remembered how out of place he had felt, timid and afraid of going out to preach his message to these strangers. He had been brought up on the stories of how Peter and Paul had entered Rome, and immediately started preaching and making converts. His own grandfather had told him stories that he had been told by his father, Septimus' great grandfather, who had actually been present at the time, and had related to him vivid accounts of the stir caused in the capital by the apostles. He had also listened many times to stories of his own hero, James, who had been sent to these same Iberians, ones reputably even fiercer in the far north of the country, and the impact that he had made there. It had, however, been days after his arrival in the village before he had felt able to go out and stand in the small market place to make his own declaration. A declaration that had been ignored at that time, he thought ruefully.

The pagus, unlike Malaca, was not a busy bustling centre, but a small hard working community of peasants who had appeared at first sight to be dour, withdrawn and even hostile in their attitudes. He was therefore startled early one morning when he was woken by the loud beat of drums, the shrill tones of flutes and the clashing of cymbals. Looking out in some alarm, he saw the street filled with people, laughing and singing, passing by in procession. He had followed them out of the village to a vineyard where they had gathered. Here they had sprinkled some of last year's wine on to the ground, drinking much more of it themselves. It was a feast to Bacchus, the God of wine, he had discovered later. This one was held at the end of vine pruning to encourage new growth. Later in the year, a second feast would be held to celebrate the harvest and the new batch of wine. All that day and into the night the festivities had continued and he had joined in, and made his first inroads into village life.

Looking back, he saw now that that had been the first step of his mission, when he was accepted by the locals. It was also when he had first met Irenus, who was to become in time his wife, and her family his first converts.

The real breakthrough though, he admitted, had been the arrival in the village of Ulpius, who he had not seen since they had both disembarked at Malaca after the voyage from Rome. One evening, his friend from the boat journey had turned up at his house, banging at his door and bellowing out his name. His surprise and delight at seeing Ulpius again was matched by his mystification as to why he was here. Ulpius would only say that he had come looking for his friend to see how the 'little father' was doing in his mission. It was years before Septimus was able to put together a satisfactory account of Ulpius' history from snippets dropped by him from time to time.

He had, apparently, originated from Gades, and had been a street urchin. At the age of 15, he had got into serious trouble over the stabbing of another youth. He had then worked his passage on a trading vessel going to Rome, and so escaped the local Gades authorities. In Rome, he had prospered as a musician, until once more coming into conflict with authority as a member of a street gang involved in robbery. He had had sufficient money to buy his passage to Malaca to once more keep ahead of the law. It was on this journey that he had met up with Septimus. All had gone well in Malaca, and he was easily able to make enough money to keep himself. Then, one day he was spotted in the street by a citizen from Gades, in Malaca on business. Fearing a new pursuit, Ulpius had gone to the bishop and found out where Septimus was living, and had made a hasty retreat into the hills to visit him. Like Septimus himself, Ulpius was never again to leave the pagus for any length of time, but was to live out his years there.

Ulpius had soon become a favourite in the village because of his lute playing and, even though he was a confirmed atheist, he played for Septimus at his daily preaching sessions, helping to gather a crowd around them. At last, Septimus was able to combine the Christian feasts with the local ones, at times such as Easter, Whitsun and Christmas. He was also able to initiate a new feast to Mary, Jesus' mother, and combine it with the summer wine feast of Bacchus.

Musing in the warm winter sun, he thought back to the high points of his work in the village. The day the headman had converted, for instance, bringing the majority of the villagers with him. The first baby girl to be christened María, after the Virgin, and the baby boys that followed, some called Angel or Serafín, later others such as Pedro and Iago after the disciples, and some even Jesús after the Lord himself.

Then there was the day that the village headman had come to him and told him that the congregation wanted him to give up his job as clerk, and that they themselves would support him as a full time deacon. By that time, he had been married to Irenus for a good while and they had inherited some of her family's land. The fruits of this land, together with the stipend offered, were enough to live on, and he had accepted their offer gladly.

His crowning achievement, in his own eyes, was when one of the young men of the village, Esteban, who he had baptised himself in the name of the first martyr Steven, the one persecuted by Paul himself before his conversion, went to Malaca to study to be a deacon. Esteban was now back in the village and had been at first his assistant, until just last year when he himself, having finally retired, had handed over the post fully to the youngster. "He'd been doing it for years anyway," the old man admitted to himself, reflecting how he had progressively handed over all his duties, doing less and less himself as he got older.

And now, the old man mused, there was all this change. New words such as priest and Pope. New pressures, such as trying to make all deacons and priests celibate. There were new writings too, more comprehensive than the original two scrolls he had brought with him. Two of these had made their way to the village in recent years, one said to be based on the writings and words of the disciple Matthew, and the other on those of the early apostle and friend of Paul, Mark. These new scrolls he welcomed, however, unlike many of the other new innovations. There was still much argument in the Church between those rooted in Judaism who wished all Christians to accept Jewish teachings and law, and those based on the joint teachings of Peter and Paul, who insisted on a wider approach open to all. There was even much talk of a schism by a Greek philosophic group, who claimed that Jesus had not been a man at all. News was also spreading of a fresh wave of persecution against the Church in Rome.

He sighed and settled back once again. It was all too much for him now, he was too old to be a martyr, too set in his ways to change, too timid, he acknowledged, to stand up for one faction or another. Let others cry heretic and shout and fight, he thought. He may have compromised with both Bacchus and Mithras, and joined forces with the village pagan cults; his mission may have started slowly and may not have caused a stir in the village, only a feast day could do that, he wryly thought, but he had succeeded in the end. The people now believed, followed the new God, the only God he told himself sternly, and were slowly forgetting the old ways.

Beside him, Ulpius awoke from his doze, breaking into his musings.

"Well, little father," he said. "Is it time to go and have a little of this blood of your God?"

"Some wine of your Bacchus?" Septimus replied in return.

"Not my Bacchus, old friend, I'll have no God in my life at all, yours or anyone's," came the good natured answer.

"Time enough anyway for a glass before eating, you old sinner," countered Septimus.

The two old men got to their feet and started off together, still arguing with each other. Esteban saw them coming as he came out of the small church Septimus had had built and dedicated to *St. Andreas,* Andrew, rather than to Iago who he would have preferred, and who was his own mentor.

"He is a humble man," thought Esteban, "and would not even force his own choice on to the village, simply accepting their preference." He greeted the two old men with a smile. Roman citizen and vagabond they may both have been, Christian and unbeliever they may both be. But despite this they were, he knew, firm friends and wherever they may have come from, and by whatever routes they may have followed, they were now both at home, here in the village.

42

"*Vaya Usted con Dios,* go with God," he greeted them as they passed, receiving in return a smile from one and a snort, albeit accompanied with twinkling eyes, from the other.

CHAPTER 5

ESPAÑA GÓTICA
(GOTHIC SPAIN)

The Gothic era in Spain started with the decline of the Roman Empire, and the arrival in 409 AD of several northern and Teutonic tribes. These were made up of the Swabians, the Vandals and the Visigoths. They ruled the indigenous population of Spain but were far fewer in number. During their time, there was never a fully stable situation in the peninsula. They conquered the whole of it (bar an area in the north) but did not have it fully under their control until 624 AD. They brought their own Arian form of Christianity, whilst much of the Hispanic population still adhered to the Catholicism associated with the previous Roman rulers.

The instability of this era was added to by the frequency with which the Gothic Kings were changed, most being displaced by murder. Many of the heirs to the throne were also disposed of before they could be enthroned. The order of succession was always in dispute, and changed from being hereditary to being subject to election as factions gained the upper hand.

In southern Spain, an area around the ports of Málaga and Cartagena was reconquered for a period by a Roman force, as were some of the offshore islands. This Byzantine enclave however only lasted for a few years before once more being restored to Gothic control.

There was much tension between these 'barbaric' new overlords, who were generally looked on with disdain by the vanquished majority population of Hispanics and Romans. The Hispanics regarded the invaders as uncouth barbarians, whilst they in their turn considered the indigenous populace to be backward peasantry.

The Goths also brought with them harsh punishments for crimes such as theft, homosexuality, rape, tampering with official documents, magic, witchcraft, spell making and the practice of bringing down curses on men, crops, animals and so forth.

Such punishments included ordeals by ducking stool, amputation of limbs, whipping, castration, head shaving, burning at the stake and death by other various ways. These punishments were bitterly resented by the Hispanic majority who, especially in the cities, were more liberal and anarchic in their lifestyle. Even in the more backward and less educated country areas, there was also resentment and unrest by the sturdily independent locals. In these more remote country areas, pagan rituals and practices were still carried out alongside the official Christian ones. Lewd dances and bawdy singing featured in many of the festivals and fiestas, especially in the more remote areas. Both communities, Gothic and Hispanic, tended to live separately and followed their own ways. The Goths thought the rural Spanish lascivious, lustful, smutty and obscene ignorant peasants. The ruling Goths, smaller in number, were considered to be wild, long-haired and intolerant savages. It didn't lend itself to a stable state of affairs.

This instability of the Gothic rule was compounded by the continual menace to the north from the Byzantine forces, and from the south by the threat of the Moorish kingdoms.

It was from the south that the eventual fall of Gothic Spain was to come in 711 AD, when Arab Tariq invaded from Tangiers. He was helped in this by the Spaniards Count Julian and the Bishop of Sevilla, who were both plotting against the latest Gothic King, Frederick.

The time of the Goths was short in the history of the Iberian Peninsula, lasting from 409 AD until 711 AD. The Moorish advance was fairly rapid, and by 910 AD they occupied the entire region with the exception of the far north. Here the Byzantine Empire prevailed, and managed to stop the Arabé forces and begin the slow process of the reconquest. The time of the Goths was over, they had already been removed from Europe and now had been overrun in Spain which they had made their main kingdom. They left behind them very few signs of their stay in the country. Nothing of architectural note and little of their culture, save a few jewellery trinkets. Fortunately, they didn't destroy much of the Roman legacy they had inherited either.

In the pueblo, a small group of Goths were in charge of the original inhabitants, who were a mixture of local Spanish, and Romans who

45

had stayed after the collapse of the Empire, together with ex-slaves from many places. These locals were hard to tell apart, and in fact because of inter breeding over the centuries most were of mixed race and blood.

◊   ◊   ◊   ◊   ◊

Alaric didn't like being disturbed in the middle of the night, especially when he had retired late with a skin full of ale and a belly full of food. He came slowly awake, realising that Gailavera, his wife, was shaking his arm.

"Ugh," he said, mouth dry, head throbbing and an acid taste rising in his gullet. "What is it, woman?"

Gailavera, who was in a similar state to her husband and who had been wakened by her maid, Brenhilda, was in no mood to entertain his bad temper. "Wake up, Alaric, there's trouble in the village. Tulga is waiting for you in the next room."

Alaric was the Gothic Lord of the Hispanic mountain village high up in the sierras, not far from the Mediterranean Sea. The village that is central to this story. Tulga was his lieutenant, leader of the small group of soldiers under his command.

Flinging aside the bed coverings and in so doing uncovering the naked body of his wife, he stumbled out of bed. Gailavera shouted a curse after his retreating body and pulled the covers back over her. Still dressing, her husband pushed past the servant Brenhilda, asking what time it was.

"Not yet cockcrow," she answered, eyeing his half-dressed body with gleaming and knowing eyes. Alaric was a tall, broad shouldered man with long flaxen hair, typical of the North European tribe he came from. Feeling her eyes on him, and remembering their dalliance of two days ago, he hurried past her. She was slim and almost as tall as he and had a well developed figure, even half awake with bedraggled hair and hastily dressed she was still an attractive and alluring woman. She knew this, and knew also that Alaric was well aware of her as he brushed past.

Tulga was waiting beyond the door, fully dressed, with a sword in his hand and a helmet on his head. He too recognised her attractions but preferred those of Gailavera, whose fuller body he had glimpsed through the open door when Alaric had left the bed. He was much shorter than Alaric, sturdy and strongly built and with little imagination or ambitions of his own. He was an ideal second in command. Quickly he outlined the problem to his irate and not fully awake master.

It was late august and the village was in the midst of the feast of the grape. The feast that was dedicated to the end of the harvest by the local catholic priest Alex, and by the villagers to the Christian God, but also with the vestiges of the old celebrations to Bacchus. The event was also celebrated by the Goths, led by the Arian priest, Tius. It was the dinner given by Alaric following this Arian worship that had resulted in his present hung-over state.

The grapes were in and the first wine already made. Two days of feasting and drinking had already taken place in the village, the festivities lasting until dawn. Tulga explained that in the middle of last night, just a few hours before, two of his soldiers who were keeping watch on the proceedings had tried to break up a group of villagers dancing naked round an image of Bacchus, led by one Olalla. Olalla was a young nubile local who Tius, the Gothic priest, had accused more than once of being a witch, and of casting spells on members of his congregation, made up of local Goths who worshipped in the Arian not the Roman church.

Tulga also told Alaric that when the soldiers had tried to break up the revellers, a drunken brawl had broken out between them and all of the villagers. More soldiers and locals had joined the fray, heads were broken and several inhabitants of the pueblo taken into custody, including Olalla herself. Tulga went on to tell him that Goncalo, the local Spanish mayor, together with Pedro, were waiting to see him in the small Gothic fort, along with several villagers. Pedro was the local Spanish administrator who ran the small council led by Goncalo, the mayor. He was also the link man who was used by Alaric in his dealings with the village council. A small swarthy black-haired local Spaniard, Pedro was a born organiser and peacemaker. He was also a

47

close friend of Tulga, which helped in sorting out problems between the two races. What Tulga didn't tell his master was that Liuva, Alaric's daughter, had also been discovered at the fiesta in the arms of a local Spaniard, he hoped that he could keep this bit of scandal away from Alaric. The soldier who had literally stumbled upon them entwined together at the edge of the plaza had been sworn to secrecy by Tulga, on pain of death.

Alaric and Tulga came out of the house and made their way to the fort, just as the first cocks were beginning to crow. Alaric had downed a flagon of small beer just before leaving, handed to him by Brenhilda with a provocative smile.

Their route took them through the village, a collection of quite primitive stone houses roughly rendered and thatched with the local esparto grass. Here and there were more modern dwellings, mainly those built by the Goths.

The fort was adapted from the one left behind by the Romans, and stood on a low hill overlooking the village. The Romans had built their barracks on the site of an earlier Bronze Age fortification, just as the Moors would also ultimately do on the ruins of the present one.

When the two men reached the fort, they were met by a scrum of people: Goncalo, who had been joined by his wife, Ynes, and the priest, Alex, at the head of about ten locals on the one hand, and Wamba, Dag and Egica and several others of Tulga's soldiers and Tius the Arian priest on the other. The small courtyard in the centre of the fort was a bedlam of voices.

Order was at last restored, and Pedro was tasked with trying to sort out the chaos. After a consultation with both parties, he was able to come to a list of the charges that the soldiers wanted brought against some of the residents of the village.

"There seems," he told Alaric and Goncalo, the two civic leaders, "to be a general charge of riot against a group of people, plus separate charges against certain individuals. Olalla is charged with lewd activity, namely dancing naked in the village square, and of witchcraft. The solder Dag said she cast a spell on him when he took her into custody. She, by the way, accuses him of handling her...... ah.... breasts and ....um... private parts, shall I say, when bringing her in."

There was a pause in his report, and Olalla could be indistinctly heard from inside the cell where she'd been put, shouting, "Private parts be damned, he put his fingers into my...." The last words were muffled as a soldier in the cell clamped a hand over her mouth.

"Yes, well," Pedro continued. "Jacobo is accused of hitting a soldier with a rock and splitting open his skull. The soldier is still unconscious, but the doctor thinks there will be no lasting damage. Diego is, along with Olalla, accused of dancing naked, he is the only other reveller to be caught by the soldiers." Pedro paused again and cleared his throat. "On the other hand, Teresa accuses Egico, one of the soldiers, of stripping and raping her. He, for his part, claims she was already naked, as she was one of the dancers. He says that it wasn't rape, but that she encouraged him."

"Is that the end of it?" Alaric asked and, on being told it was, breathed a sigh of relief. It was bad enough, and Tulga had informed him that feelings on both sides were running high and the air was tense. The last thing he wanted was a riot on his hands. Olalla had several times come close to being charged with pagan practices and witchcraft, for which the penalty could be trial by either water or fire. Ducking or burning at the stake, death the result in either event. On the other hand, she was an attractive young woman and had more than once caught his eye. It would, he mused, be a waste to drown or burn her; it could be amusing to try and tame her, lay claim to her obvious charms. He caught the eye of Tius, the stern Arian priest, at this point and shut all thoughts of Olalla out of his mind.

If the soldier didn't die, then a charge of assault during a skirmish could be overlooked. And then the rape, if Teresa were one of the nude dancers then surely she could be persuaded to drop the charge. The last thing he wanted was for the tension to mount, perhaps for a riot to take place. Things in the region were unsettled enough, and his superiors on the coast would not look kindly on him if he lost control of his village.

Alaric turned to his lieutenant Tulga, the local leader Goncalo and Pedro the peacemaker.

"Shall we go into the fort, have a few mouthfuls of food, perhaps a flask or two of ale or wine, and try to work out a solution to this mess?

I am certainly in need of sustenance. We were all celebrating a good harvest yesterday, you with your fiesta and us at a dinner at my manor house. Things got a bit heated and out of hand, but surely we can work out a solution. We don't want to spoil the last day of the feast, do we?"

With daylight came sore heads, remorse and a wish on both sides to smooth things over, aided and abetted by the efforts of the two local leaders, their immediate henchmen and above all by Pedro. That and the desire by both sides to enjoy the final day of the feast of the grape. The heat of the morning sun was also spreading drowsiness over the already tired and hung-over crowd. Passions had cooled as the sun warmed their bodies and dulled their senses. The doors of the cells were opened and all the detainees allowed to return home, after stern cautions all round. Olalla emerged decently and modestly clothed in a soldier's tunic, her own clothes not having been found anywhere in the village square, despite a search by two of the soldiers.

As the cell doors opened, so too did the eyes of the soldier hit with a rock. He sat up and was violently sick over the doctor attending him. He then asked where he was and what had happened. His helmet had taken most of the force out of the blow and he was soon up and bore Jacobo, who he knew well, no bad feelings. The mild concussion he was suffering from would be short-lived.

It was a good result all round, Alaric thought, as he returned home. When he got there, he was met with the news that Gailavera, his wife, had ridden off to a nearby village to visit friends and would not be back until early evening. Gratefully, he returned to his bed to catch up on his lost sleep. He was thwarted in this when the lithe body of Brenhilda, his wife's maid, slipped in beside him. At last he slept, after he had satisfied her several times over in the next couple of hours, and she finally left him in peace. She was a demanding woman and hard to please, especially in his present state of exhaustion.

Sleep and peace came at last to his overtired mind and body, along with harmony in his village and his life. His last thought, after Brenhilda left his bed, was the hope that the final night of the feast of the grape would pass off in reasonable tranquillity; Goth and Spaniard celebrating separately and together in harmony.

He would not have slept so contentedly if he had known that Gailavera had not gone to visit friends, or at least not the kind of friends he had envisaged on being told of her excursion. The single friend who she had gone to visit was in fact Giler, a Goth of noble birth in a nearby village, and her lover.

He would also not have slept so easy if he had known that Liuva, his teenage daughter, had also gone out to visit a lover, this time local Spaniard Bernal, one of Goncalo's councillors, and the one she had been caught with the previous night.

Olalla, who had caught his eyes and his imagination, was also helping to break down the separation of the two races, by having an assignation with another of his soldiers, Linva.

Thankfully, he knew nothing of these exploits and so thought that life in the pueblo went on peacefully as he slept.

CHAPTER 6

MOROS Y CRISTIANOS
(Moors and Christians)

In July of 710 AD the Arab ruler of North Africa, Bey Mūsā ibn Nusayr, sent a raiding party of four hundred men under the leadership of Tarīf, one of the lieutenants of the Emir, Tāriq ibn Ziyād of Tangiers. They had landed at the southernmost tip of Hispania to the west of Calpe (Gibraltar), and after a short stay had brought back both booty and captives. In this venture he had the support of Count Julian. The Count was the Masīhī (Christian) ruler of Septum (Ceuta) at that time. Julian had encouraged Mūsā to invade the Spanish mainland in reply to the alleged rape of his daughter by the Spanish King, Roderick. The Bey was also supported by and had made an allegiance with two local Hispanic leaders, Achila, son of the previous king who had pretentions to the throne, and the bishop of Sevilla who supported this claim. Both of them promised Mūsā to supply men to support any further army he might send.

Mūsā had been so pleased with the success of this venture that he named the point on the coast at which Tarif had landed Tarifa, as it is still called today. He also decided to send a bigger expedition the following year, this time under the command of the Emir himself, Tāriq ibn Ziyād.

In April 711 AD, the invading army boarded the boats provided by Count Julian for the attack. The force of seven thousand men, mostly Berbers, landed in the bay next to Calpe (at what is now Algeciras) and established a base. The mount of Calpe, one of the two pillars of Hercules, beside which he landed, has since then been called Jabel Tāriq, the mount of Tāriq (which is now perpetuated in the name Gibraltar, the height of Gibra).

This was the beginning of the conquest of most of Spain which was to last for many centuries.

◊   ◊   ◊   ◊   ◊

The voice of the Muezzin came faintly over the air to the group of men working on the hilltop.

"God is the great. God is the great.

God is the great. God is the great.

I do testify that there is no deity save God ...."

The Muezzin was an old man and, as yet, there was no minaret in the pueblo, so he was not raised very high off the ground. His voice came faintly and barely audible to them as they laboured. The men stopped working and the Moslems amongst them moved to one side, and spread their mats on the ground in preparation for prayer.

The two overseers of the workmen broke off their conversation, and looked across to the lower hilltop at the Muezzin standing on his low stone column which had been built for him.

The taller of the two overseers, Karim ibn Rushd, dark-complexioned with black hair and long straggling beard, turned back to his companion. He pointed towards the lower hill with his right hand, from which two fingers were missing.

"It's midday prayer, I'll go to the Mescit (small Mosque) and return here after I've worshipped, and then eaten."

The second man smiled back. The Mescit only existed in the imagination of his partner at present. It would not be built until the fort they were erecting here was finished.

"Right," he answered. "I'll keep this lot going until you get back."

He turned and, limping slightly, made his way to the group of Christians who were still working, whilst their Moslem colleagues were getting ready to make their midday prayers.

The men were building the main walls of the fort, and had reached a height of about two metres. The remaining overseer, Enrique Larra y Caballero, climbed up on to the wooden scaffolding to join the masons and, glancing across the pueblo, he saw the figure of Karim reach the Imam and the group of worshippers gathered around him.

"Karim ibn Rushd," he thought. "My old enemy, and now my good friend, going to pray to his God. How things change, a few years ago we'd never met, then we fought, and now...... now we are friends and work together."

Some years previously Karim, a Berber, had been living in Tangiers close to Septum (Ceuta) on the North African coast. He was a Captain in the army of the Emir, Tāriq ibn Ziyād. Septum had a Masīhī (Christian) ruler at that time, Count Julian. Julian had just returned to Africa from Hispania where he had been to bring back his daughter, Florianda, from Toledo where she had been a student. Rumours flew around the Christian enclave of Septum, reaching the Moors living nearby. It was said that Roderick, the Hispanic King, had raped Florianda when she was bathing in the river Tajo. Karim did not know if this was true or not, but he did know that shortly after his return with his daughter, Count Julian had had a meeting with the Arab ruler of North Africa, Bey Mūsā ibn Nusayr. At this meeting, the enraged Julian had apparently told the Bey that Roderick had asked Julian to send him a present of some African hawks.

"I told him I would send him such hawks that he could never have envisaged," Julian was rumoured to have said. He then encouraged the Bey to attack Hispania, promising him the help of certain locals on the mainland and also holding out the prospect of much plunder.

Whatever the truth of these stories, the Bey sent a raiding party of four hundred men under the leadership of Tarīf, one of Tāriq ibn Ziyād's lieutenants. They had landed at the southernmost tip of Hispania to the west of Calpe (Gibraltar), and after a short stay had brought back both booty and captives, amongst them many beautiful women. They had also made a pact with some local leaders who had promised to join them after they had landed.

Mūsā decided to send a bigger expedition the following year, this time under the command of the Emir himself, Tāriq ibn Ziyād. Karim, as a captain in Tāriq's army, had then been involved in the proceedings and joined the force that was being assembled for the invasion. He, along with his men, boarded the boats provided by Count Julian for the attack. The force landed in the bay next to Calpe and established a base.

Enrique, at this time, had been peacefully living in the pueblo, some way to the east of these events. When he heard of the invasion, King Roderick, who was in the north of the country, had sent messengers far and wide calling for men to join his army, before starting off for the south.

In Hispania in those days, each man owed allegiance directly to the King himself, not to a local leader who could commit their service to the ruler. So, when the summons reached the pueblo, each man had to decide for himself whether to answer the call or not. The King's call to arms got a mixed reception in the village, as it did in much of the area. It was April, and there was much work to be done on the land. The rumours of Roderick's rape of Florianda had also reached them, and there was a lot of disapproval of him for this. Some in the pueblo preferred Achila over Roderick, and supported his claim to the throne. Why, many argued, should they rally to his standard to fight these invading forces? Others however, Enrique included, had resented the incursion of the Islamic troops and were bored with rural life. They wanted action and a change from farming, and decided to go to the King's aid. A party of eight villagers, Enrique heading them, had set out to journey to Gades (Cádiz), which was Roderick's rallying point. En route, they added to their number with more volunteers from other villages of the region.

At Calpe, Tāriq was joined by Achila and the bishop of Sevilla with their men. This combined force of Moors and Christians moved westwards towards Gades. In Gades, Roderick, newly arrived from the north with his own army, was organising them and the many others who had flocked to his standard. As soon as he thought that he had enough troops, he led his men to the east to meet up with the Moors.

The armies of the *Moros y Cristianos*, Moors and Christians, were destined to meet up in the marshy wadi (valley) in the delta of the River Barbate (between what is now Vejer and Alcalá de los Gazules) on the 19th of July. On that morning Roderick, at the head of his men, saw the Moors crossing the marshy valley below him as he paused on the low hills to the west of the valley. Quickly, he lined up his troops and charged down on the enemy. Tāriq's army had been augmented not only by Achila and his men, but also with a further five thousand Berbers sent from Tangiers, and to add to Roderick's problems, many of his troops became disaffected and withdrew from the battlefield. The battle raged all morning, with the Moors gaining the upper hand.

The two small companies, led by Enrique and Karim, met each other in the marshy wastes beside a narrow stream in the delta in the early afternoon, when the battle was nearing its conclusion. Both groups were by then tired and had suffered many casualties, and had been in the process of withdrawing from the field. They faced each other, men and animals standing ankle deep in water, across the small watercourse. Neither group were willing to fight any more as the main battle was nearly over and was, in any case, some distance away. In the end, the two captains moved forward, watched by the rest of their men. Both men dismounted and drew their swords. Karim was by far the taller of the two, but Enrique was solidly built and a born fighter, and so they were well matched. Circling, they tried to disable each other, before rushing in with savage sweeps of their weapons. For half an hour, they thrust and parried, hacked and cut, neither however landing more than glancing blows on the other. Their weary followers had watched, passively squatting either side of the stream, as their champions strove to overcome each other.

The end came quickly and dramatically. Karim, sweeping hard and low, caught Enrique a blow across the top of his thigh, cutting through his tough leather trousers and opening a deep wound. The low stroke had however left his hand vulnerable to Enrique's sword, which chopped down even as the blow struck his thigh, cutting off two of Karim's fingers and causing him to drop his sword. Two of Karim's soldiers then sprang forward to protect him from Enrique, who had leant on his sword and stood swaying, before collapsing to the ground. The two Moors then moved forward to kill him as he lay, blood pouring from his wound. The Christian soldiers began to rise to protect their captain.

"Stop," roared Karim, hurriedly wrapping a cloth around his hand to stem the flow of blood. "Leave the Masihi, is he too not a man of the book, and a brave fighter. Whilst curs like you sit and watch like women, he fought long and well, and look," he held his hand high, the red stained cloth slowly dripping blood. "Look, he gave as good as he got. Bind his wound and put a tourniquet on my arm."

All the men, Christians and Moors, gathered around the two combatants to attend to their wounds. All signs of battle had completely vanished, and from far off came the sounds of the exultant shouts from the victorious Moors.

"Go with God," Karim told the band of Christians as he led his own men in the direction of the sounds of rejoicing. When they arrived, they found the Moors surrounding the white stallion Roderick had been riding. The horse was mud spattered and still carried a saddle adorned with gold and precious stones, but of Roderick himself there was no trace. Some of the Berbers claimed to have seen the King limping away from the fray badly wounded, whilst others swore they had seen him sinking below the waters of the river.

Whatever the truth, he was never seen again. A rumour spread amongst the two armies that Roderick had escaped from the battlefield severely wounded, and had been taken by some of his men to a hermit living in a cave in the nearby hills and left in his care.

Tāriq, the following morning, started the trek north towards Córdoba to continue his conquest. He left behind a sizable body of men with instructions to spread out through the whole of southern Hispania and occupy the towns and villages of the area. Soon, they had been told, many more Moors would be crossing the straits, bringing with them their families to settle in this new land, which he had called al-Andalus. This name he derived from the present one of 'Vandalicia', land of the Vandals. Karim, because of his injuries, had been one of the group left behind to carry out the task of occupying the surrounding lands. After a delay to allow his hand to heal, he had set out eastwards at the head of one of the companies allotted to this duty.

After the fight, Enrique was carried from the field by his supporters who began their long journey home. Towards nightfall, the only two other survivors from the pueblo had been left with him, and the remainder had gone their own ways. Progress had been slow because of his wound, and as darkness fell they had found themselves only as far as the hills overlooking Calpe.

In the gloom they came upon a small cave, home of a hermit, who was tending another wounded man. With awe, the three men from the pueblo recognised their King, Roderick, who was clearly dying from his wounds. The old hermit took the last confession of the King and granted him absolution, before turning to Enrique to tend his wounded thigh. The hermit examined the wound, whilst Enrique's companions buried their King. They made a rough cross out of wood which they put on the grave, but otherwise they left it unmarked. The hermit washed Enrique's wound with a solution made from acorn cups, and then covered it with a paste of olive oil and cabbage leaves. Enrique had a high fever for a few days, for which the hermit had given him doses of a brew of garlic, yarrow, beer and honey, and his temperature had at last subsided after a brief crisis. The hermit was more successful with his second patient than he had been with his first, the King. Several days later, Enrique was able to walk again without the aid of his two friends.

The three men then continued their journey and made their slow way back to the pueblo. Of the eight who had left the village to answer Roderick's summons, only these three returned. Enrique himself was to limp for the rest of his life as a result of his wound.

Karim, in the meantime, because of his own injury, led one of the last groups making their way eastward. In each village and town that he reached on his journey, he found that they had already been occupied by earlier bands of Moors. He arrived at last at Mainake (Vélez-Málaga) and turned inland. He and his men entered the pueblo on the last day of October 711 AD, which had been the first day of a two week wet spell. The rain was falling in torrents as Karim and Enrique once more faced each other at the head of their respective groups of men. This time, however, they had greeted each other with surprised smiles of recognition. Enrique took Karim into his own house to shelter, and persuaded the villagers to take in all the other strangers.

From that time, the two men had worked together to develop the pueblo. Karim's priorities had been clear from the start. His first task had been to build houses for the Moorish immigrant families, his own included. The Moors were gardeners and the new dwellings had been built around courtyards in which plants and fountains had been placed. The local Christians had looked with interest at these buildings in the new *barrio,* district, which was being erected next to their own.

In future years, many of the original inhabitants were to copy this style of construction.

Since the time of the Romans, who had developed much of the infrastructure of the village, it had stagnated or even regressed under Visigothic rule. In their time, the Romans had built roads and bridges and a network of irrigation channels, many of which were now neglected. The Moors, under Karim, repaired and extended these, at the same time as they built their new homes. Whilst the Roman structures were functional in style, the Moors built more ornately and decoratively. The settlers also brought with them many new plants including almonds and citrus fruits, which they planted on the surrounding hills.

Karim's next priority was the construction of a small fort on the hill overlooking the village, on the site of the now derelict Roman one. If he had wanted to and had known where to look, he would have found evidence of the Bronze Age fort that predated the Roman one.

The construction of this fort was the task on which both Karim and Enrique were now engaged. Karim had had to insist on this priority in the face of the demands of the newly arrived Imam and Muezzin, both of whom wanted him to build a Mosque. Karim had been supported in his decision to build the fort by a Hafiz (one who has memorised the Koran) in the village, who as a scholar was looked up to by all the Moslems. His judgement had been, "First the people must have homes and then defence against the unbeliever. We can worship Allah in the open as did the prophet Muhammad, peace and honour on his name, before us. All we need is a small tower, a column of stone for the Muezzin to stand on to call the hours of prayer. Later, when the fort is completed, we can build a Mescit of great beauty next to the small Christian church on the top of the smaller hill. Then both faiths of the book can worship side by side, as the people also live side by side."

The opinions of Karim and the Hafiz had carried the day, and now the walls of the fort were rising above the pueblo. These were peaceful and prosperous days in the village after the steady decline in the times of the Visigoths. The rule of the Umayya family, from whom the 'khalīfa' (Caliphe) came, was an enlightened one. Both Christians and Jews were allowed religious and social freedom, and given protection by their Moslem rulers. The Moors brought with them learning and new ideas. The intellectual life in al-Andalus flowered, and there were many advances in art and architecture, as well as progress in both agriculture and science.

The friendship between Karim and Enrique, and the regeneration of the pueblo, mirrored in a small way the transformation of the whole peninsula and its inhabitants, both *Moros y Cristianos.*

CHAPTER 7

ESPAÑA ÁRABE
(MOORISH SPAIN)

For over 700 years, from 711 to 1492, Spain, or at least a portion of the country, was occupied by the Moors. From their initial toehold in the area around Gibraltar, they advanced until all but the very north of the Iberian Peninsula was under their control. One of the reasons why the Basque region was opposed to the Nationalist forces in the Civil War was because Franco brought his Moorish troops into the region which had not been occupied by them during those years of Árabe conquest. The pueblo at the heart of this history was in an area that was one of the first to be overrun, and the last to be freed from the invaders.

The history of the occupation was complex in nature and does not, in its detail, concern this story so a short and simplified account is all that is needed. The 780 years can be divided into three general phases.

The first was immediately after the initial landings. During these early years, various Moorish families ruled portions of the land conquered. These were usually amenable to the local inhabitants, and indeed had often been helped by them to advance into the country.

These arrangements between the various families and the locals were then overturned by the arrival of the Almoravids, dark-skinned nomads from the Sahara, who were instrumental in pushing the local forces further northwards. These forces were far stricter than the caliphates they replaced, and saw the local Christians and Jews as corrupt. The more easy going life was replaced by a more hostile regime. Many of the original Moorish settlers, mainly Berbers, also suffered under the yoke of the Almovarids, and several uprisings against their rule took place.

The third phase was the overrunning of the previous regime by another wave of Moors, the Almohads. This was a fanatical sect of mainly Shiite Moslems from the Atlas Mountains in Morocco. This invasion took place at about 1126 AD, and was extremely hostile to not only the Christians and Jews, but also the previous Moorish establishment in the now rapidly shrinking area of the peninsula in their hands. Decrees went out for churches and synagogues to be destroyed, and Christians and Jews either to adopt the Muslim faith or flee the area. Failure to do so would result in death. This hardened attitude drove the reconquest to a new height, and many northern Europeans and British soldiers joined the Spanish ranks.

In fact, many of the Moors who had already settled in Spain, especially in the southern area of al-Andalus, many of them Berbers, defied these orders. The original invading forces had not brought many women with them and intermarriage was common, so a network of family connections added to the reluctance on the part of many of the Moors to force the indigenous population to either flee to northern Christian Spain, or to slay those who refused.

The rule of the Empire virtually ended in 1212 AD, when the Moors were defeated at Toledo by a combined Spanish and European army. The Moorish commander drank himself to death after the battle, and thousands of the Moors fled back to North Africa. It was not long before the occupied area of Spain shrank to just the south of the peninsula, to what is now known as Andalucía. Here the frontier was to remain fairly static, with just minor skirmishes between the two sides until the final push by Isabella and Ferdinand in the early 1400's.

During this time al-Andalus was ruled from Granada by the Nasrid dynasty. Once more Christian and Jews were tolerated, with only minor persecutions taking place.

In the pueblo, a sizeable number of Christians remained through all the occupations, enough certainly to engage in the fierce battle that was to finally rid it of the Moors (as we shall see in the next chapter).

◊ ◊ ◊ ◊ ◊

The late afternoon sun, fierce and hot, angled down into the eastern half of the central courtyard. In the shaded area, under the added protection of a mimosa tree, Ali-Tūman sat brooding. In the centre of the patio a fountain, fed by piped water brought down from the hill above, tinkled and splashed into a small pond. All was tranquil, but Ali's thoughts were troubled. He had learnt that the Nasrid ruler in Granada was sending an envoy into the region to assess the situation viz-a-viz the Árabe and Christian communities in the villages. Tensions were running high in the frontier areas, and rumours of a fresh crusade against al-Andalus to reclaim it for Spain were in the offing. The rulers of al-Andalus wanted to be sure that the local Christians were firmly under control and unarmed.

Ali was the local headman, as his father had been before him and his grandfather. It was a local dynasty that stretched back many generations. The family had prospered with the growth of the silk industry locally. He was originally of Berber stock, now much diluted by intermarriage between his forefathers with many differing Muslims from successive waves of immigrants, but also with local Christians. His family had always been mainly tolerant of their conquered neighbours, and sometimes it was not easy to tell which families were of which religion. Now, however, tensions and divisions were growing and lines being drawn. The sounds of war were beginning to be heard.

If that were not bad enough, there were also splits in the two local communities as well. Hardliners on the one side and peacemakers on the other. Moors of Berber, Persian, Moroccan and other backgrounds, arguing amongst themselves, and Christians content with Ali's rule at odds with those who wanted to throw off the yoke of Islam.

These fault lines resulted in not just divisions between the two groups but also amongst themselves, setting brother against brother, and dividing families and friends. The status quo or change, war or peace, Christian or Islamic rule, these were the questions facing not just the pueblo but the whole of the region.

Ali by nature was a peacemaker. As a youth, he had served for a while near Jerez de la Frontera, and later lost a son, killed during a flare up of hostilities at Cortes de la Frontera. These experiences, together with his family's continual peaceful control of the pueblo, had produced his desire for peace. Now the Nasrids were beginning to take a hard line and demanding his compliance. The Nasrids were Shia Moslems, and despised other Islamic factions as well as infidels.

All this was bad enough, but he was also beset by family tensions and splits inside his own home. Looking around the quiet courtyard and seeing no movement, he surreptitiously slipped a small flask from below his robe and uncorking it, took a few sips of its contents. *Vino terreno,* the local wine. He relaxed as the liquid spread warmth though his body. Like many Muslims, especially the ruling class, he often drank alcohol, just like the defeated general at Toledo, who was an Almohad and a supposed religious hardliner. In Ali's case his drink was the local wine, illegally brewed by the Christians, with both his knowledge and blessing. Forbidden to use their grapes to make wine the local Christians dried them all, turning them into *pasas,* raisins, and then used a portion of these to turn into a sweet strong liqueur.

And here was another problem. Alfonso, a Christian friend, from whom he secretly bought his tipple, was becoming one of the locals amongst the growing number of those wanting freedom.

"Not that I wish any harm on you, Ali," he had told him the other day. "You could stay here, even keep this splendid house. But we need our freedom, after all these years."

Ali was an old man now, too old in his opinion for all this argument, conspiracy and trouble. He just wanted peace for the last few years of his life, and for his children.

There was a movement to one side of him as his first wife, Salma, came out of the house to bring him a cool drink of sherbet, a sweet fragrant mixture of flower essence and water. Salma was the mother of his eldest son, the one killed at Cortes, and two of his daughters, both now married and living near to Granada. His second wife had died in childbirth and Rachid, her son, was now his first heir and one of the many thorns in his flesh. His third wife, a sour and bitter woman, he had sent back to Morocco to her family, together with her two sons and three daughters. They were now constantly sending messages and demanding to be allowed to return, and also for the eldest boy to become his successor as village headman instead of Rachid. Ali, who wanted neither of them as his heir, was pinning all his hopes on Sol, his fourth wife, nineteen to his sixty-two years, to supply him with a more amenable next in line.

Salma, who was well past childbearing age, a pleasant plump woman, handed him his drink and sank down on the chair next to him. She was the only person he trusted in his household, indeed in the village, and knew all his thoughts and secrets. For a while, they sat discussing the many problems facing him. She too wanted Sol to bear him a son to take his place as the local Mudir. She had no time for Rachid. Having lost her own son, her first born, Rachid did not come anywhere up to him in her eyes. She also wanted nothing to do with Chaymas, his third wife living in Morocco, or either of her sons, who she had never liked. So she was, like Ali, looking for Sol to produce a successor. But time was running out, the Christians were gearing up for an onslaught on al-Andalus and if they succeeded, there might not be many years in hand for him to grow into a man. Also Ali was finding it difficult to put his seed into Sol even, that is, if he were still fertile.

Ali was a huge man, vastly overweight and now not capable of moving or walking any distance. He no longer left his house, in fact he seldom moved far beyond his bed chamber and the inner courtyard. He never walked the streets of the pueblo or went to the Moorish castle on the hill overlooking the village, but relied on Saad-Hāmi, its commandant, to visit him in his home to discuss military matters.

Sol, who was a slender and slight Arab beauty, was more than willing to bear him children, but found that bearing his weight was more of a problem. Normally, she pleasured him by hand or mouth whilst he was sitting in his chair or lying on his bed, and could only copulate by straddling his huge body. Yet, after months of marriage, no sign of pregnancy was to be seen.

Selma had come up with a solution unknown, she thought, to Ali. She engineered an affair between Jalal, the son of her firstborn Simo who had died at Cortes, and Sol, in the hope that if Ali did not plant his seed in Sol, Jalal would. Ali in fact knew of this, and as Jalal was his favourite grandson, was content to allow the conspiracy to continue, as long as he could also enjoy the attentions of Sol.

The following day, the emissary sent from Granada to the pueblo arrived. Ali was surprised to find that he came with only one

65

companion and guard, despite the unrest at present on the plains of the *mesa* between the sierras where the village lay, and Granada. No traveller was safe, as bands of warring Moors, outcasts, robbers and other hotheads roamed the area.

Yūsuf ibn-Rahmān, however, came with only one companion. He came over the top of the sierra by way of the track laid down originally by the Romans many centuries ago, descending by the steep track down to the hump-backed bridge over the stream at the bottom, and then up the gentle rise to the village.

Yūsuf was a hardliner, a descendant of the Almohads of Morocco, and quickly began to berate Ali for his lenient attitude towards the Christians in the pueblo. He was especially critical of Ali's friendship with Alfonso, the local Spanish headman Diago, and the priest, Ferro. For five days, Yūsuf stayed in the village, looking and listening to all that went on. He sought the views of many of the local Moors and especially of Saad, the military commandant and a well-known hardliner.

Ali knew that the report Yūsuf took back to Granada would be highly critical and would probably call for his removal, to be replaced by a sterner local ruler. If he was to retain his position, then something must be done. But what?

The day before the emissary was due to leave, Ali and Salma talked the matter over and decided on drastic measures. The emissary, they decided, must not be allowed to return to Granada and give his report.

They decided to ask Jalal, their grandson, to go ahead of the two emissaries and ambush them as they descended from the heights of the sierra above the village to the plains below. They promised him that if he succeeded in his task, he would be made guardian of any male offspring of Sol's, and rule the village after Ali's death until the youngster came of age. This would enable Ali to pass his leadership on to his descendants, as they had passed it on to him. It also meant that Jalal would be involved with Sol in bringing up his own illegitimate son. The deaths of the men from Granada would be put down to the unrest in the region.

All this, of course, depended on the Moorish state of al-Andalus lasting long enough for that prospective heir to be born and grow up. And for Sol to finally become pregnant, either through the efforts of Ali, or more likely Jalal.

Only time would tell.

CHAPTER 8

SÉ DE ELLA

(THE STORY OF HOW THE PUEBLO GOT ITS NAME)

For centuries, the Moors remained in control of much of Spain. They were slowly forced out of northern Spain, and in the end held only most of Andalucía. Then the final push came to free the land at last from their grip.

Los Reyes Cátolicos, the Catholic Kings, Isabella and Ferdinand, were making perhaps their most decisive move in the ten year struggle against the last Moorish enclave in Spain, the kingdom of Granada. Their army, gathered at Córdoba, was now in 1486 sweeping across al-Andalus by way of Antequera towards the sea port of Málaga, second city after Granada itself of the Moorish kingdom.

For several centuries, this Moorish province had co-existed, uneasily, with Christian Spain. The frontier had been forever fluid and subject to plundering of Moor on Christian, and Christian on Moor.

Antequera itself had been captured by an earlier Ferdinand, King of Spain some 80 years before the start of the current conflict, and had been held ever since as a gateway through which further inroads could occur. This capture was followed by a period of stability with the signing of a truce between the Spanish King, Enrique, and the Moorish Sultan, Mulay Aben Ismael. The Sultan, fearful of the might of Spain and conscious of the insecurity of his kingdom, had agreed to pay a tribute in gold annually to the Spanish throne to ensure peace between the two nations.

However, when his son Mulay Abul Hassan came to the throne in Granada, he had reneged on the treaty and refused to pay any more tribute. "Our mint coins nothing but blades of scimitars and heads of lances" was the message he sent to Isabella and Ferdinand via their ambassador, Don Juan de Vera, who had travelled to Granada to collect the tribute due.

Mulay Abul Hassan was a much fiercer ruler than his father and he had refused to be a puppet ruler, seeking rather to consolidate and even extend his kingdom. This refusal of tribute had been followed by a period of renewed border conflict and unrest.

A few years after Abul Hassan refused to pay any more tribute, he led an attack on the stronghold of Zahara on the border, near to the Moorish town of Ronda. The castle at Zahara, which had been considered impregnable and was only lightly garrisoned, had fallen to his forces, sending shock waves through the whole of the Spanish kingdom.

These events, and the obvious threat of another Moorish conquest of Spain under the fierce Mulay Abul Hassan, were the trigger to war which was then to break out between Isabella and Ferdinand, and the Moorish Nasrid kingdom of Granada. For years, the Catholic Kings had been struggling to hold together their kingdom which was torn with strife, struggle and tensions between the various regions and local rulers. A crusade against the infidels was what they had needed to unite the country against a common foe.

In the same year that Abul Hassan had captured the fortress of Zahara on his borders, the Marques of Cádiz led a force into the very heart of the Granada kingdom, and captured the castle and town of Alhama. This town stood almost in the centre of the kingdom of Granada, in the rich and fruitful *vega* which surrounded Granada itself, and on the main inland route between Granada city and Málaga, the two principal towns of the Moorish enclave. Despite repeated attempts to recapture the town, it was however to remain in Christian hands until the fall of Granada itself some ten years later.

Sometime after the capture of Alhama, the Marqués of Cádiz and other prominent Christian leaders had made an incursion into the western part of the Axarquía from the town of Antequera. The Axarquía is a wild and desolate area, mountainous with a maze of steep-sided valleys, which abounded with fortified towns filled with Moorish soldiers. This expedition had soon run into problems, becoming broken into small groups, each getting lost in the maze of valleys and becoming harassed by the Moorish defenders who knew every inch of the land. Eventually, they had been forced to retreat to Antequera, suffering many losses.

Isabella and Ferdinand had then taken a firm grip on the campaign, and immediately led an attack on the castle of Zahara, which they recaptured shortly after the debacle in the Axarquía.

The following year had seen a campaign in the west of the Granada kingdom which led to the capture of Ronda itself, long thought to be impregnable, but which was breached by the Spanish army's heavy artillery. After this came the capture of Coín, Cártama, Casarabonela and Marbella.

There then followed a strike to the northern borders of the Moorish kingdom which resulted in the fall of Loja and Moclin, both of which were on the edge of the *vega* surrounding Granada itself.

The Catholic Kings had then decided that it was time to cut off the kingdom's supply route to North Africa, and to attack the two large harbours of Málaga and Almería. They had therefore gathered together their army at Córdoba, and set out on Palm Sunday for Antequera en route to Málaga. The heavy artillery of cannon and slings needed for the siege were now moving slowly towards Antequera via good roads in the valleys and across the *vega*, whilst Ferdinand led the army by a more direct route crossing the hilly country standing in the way.

The direct route from Antequera to Málaga ran down the narrow twisting gorge of the river Guadalhorce where ambush would have been a constant problem, and through which the army would have had to advance as a narrow column and overcome many obstacles. Ferdinand therefore turned east behind the sierras of Málaga until reaching Zafarraya, where a pass breaks the mountain chain and an easier descent was possible to the coastal plain. This descent ran through the centre of the Axarquía, avoiding the fortified towns of Alcaucín and Viñuela to the east, and Periana and Benamargosa to the west, until it reached the large town of Vélez-Málaga near the coast. From the high pass, Ferdinand could see the *vega* and coastline below, and realised that once down to the coastal plain he would have to capture the town of Vélez-Málaga before turning to the west to confront Málaga. He led his army down the pass and encamped to the north of Vélez, between the town and the Moorish fortress of Bentomiz, which dominated a high peak overlooking Vélez.

◊ ◊ ◊ ◊ ◊

In the pueblo itself, this campaign by *Los Reyes Cátolicos* had been followed by all the inhabitants since its commencement some six years earlier. The pueblo lies in the eastern Axarquía, to the south of the Sierra Tejeda and just below its highest point, the mountain of Maroma.

Alhama is situated immediately to the north east of Maroma, and traders from the pueblo travelling to Granada passed over the high ridge to Alhama on their journey. The local economy was based on almonds, olives and grapes and these, together with salted fish from the nearby coast, were taken by mule over the hill to Granada. Traders therefore had brought the news of the fall of Alhama to the Christian forces, and since that time they had had to skirt the town on their route to Granada, often falling victim to forays from the town. The local economy was also based in part on the goat with the production of milk, cheese and meat. Large herds of these goats roamed the hills with their shepherds, and those that ventured up to the crest of the ridge were able to see the constant movements of both Christian and Moorish troops around Alhama.

The disastrous incursion of western Axarquía by the Marquéz of Cádiz had come close to the pueblo itself, and many of the Moorish warriors of the village had joined the forces opposing the invaders. And now the columns of troops converging on Vélez-Málaga were passing fairly close to the west of the pueblo, and the sound of the siege of the town could clearly be heard.

During the Moorish occupation of the pueblo, the two separate communities had co-existed in reasonable harmony for centuries; indeed there had been intermarriage between them, and conversions to Islam by some of the original Christian community. The pueblo itself was divided into two *barrios,* districts, one mainly Moorish and the other mainly Christian. A small Moorish fort overlooked the village which was under the control of a local Mudir or headman, Aben Guzman. Since the coming to the throne of Granada of Mulay Hassan, however, tension had mounted between the two parts of the town. The stern Nasrid King, Mulay Hassan, had issued a decree that all

71

Mozarabic Christians in Granada province were to be expelled. Whilst this was mainly achieved in Granada itself and in the larger towns, in the remote districts of the Axarquía and the Alpujarras, things were different. The stricter policies of the Moorish authorities had however increased the tensions between the Moorish community and their Christian neighbours. The capture of Alhama, and the disturbances in the Axarquía, had also added to this, and the presence of a large Christian army investing Vélez close by had raised the temperature even higher.

The local Mudir, Aben Guzman, had also, in recent years, brought in many strict rules and curtailed the power of the Comte who acted as a local *alcalde* or organiser of the Christian *barrio*. The priest, who operated with the unofficial blessing of the Moorish officials, had at first been prohibited from tending his congregation, and then later beheaded when he had refused to comply with their restrictions. The previously peaceful coexistence in the village broke down and neighbour turned against neighbour.

With the current advance of Ferdinand on Vélez and the news that Isabella, still in Córdoba, was raising another army to join him, Mudir Aben Guzman had begun to form the Moorish men of the pueblo into a force to either defend it against any possible attack, or to march down the hill to Vélez to help defend the besieged Moors there. He had brought together a force of over seventy well-armed and well trained men, mostly the garrison of the small fort, and almost as many again from the local peasantry.

The local Christian peasants on the other hand were both fewer in number, poorly armed, untrained and totally unorganised. They were in fact just a handful of farmers who had been in occupied territory for many, many years.

With the exception of a few who had returned to the place of their birth since the fall of Alhama, they had been ruled by the Moors all their lives. For the most part, their arms were farming implements, hunting bows and arrows, a few spears and some ancient swords. All however had knives, and the village smithy began secretly to make swords and spears.

It was one of the returners who persuaded the Comte to call a secret meeting of the younger able-bodied men to urge an attack on the Moors.

Jorge Ignacio Ruiz y Castro was a big ox of a man who had served for a while in the Spanish army of Isabella and Ferdinand, and had been present at the capture of Alhama. After the fall of Alhama Jorge, who had been injured in the leg during the battle, had returned over the mountains to the village that he had left as a child, when his family had moved to the Christian held Sevilla. He had joined the army of the Marquéz of Cádiz, who was also a *Sevillano*, Sevillian, and had taken part in the capture of Alhama.

His allegiance to the Catholic Kings was firm, especially, as with all the troops, to Isabella, a warrior queen who often rode at the head of the army. Of the two 'Kings', Ferdinand was the schemer. He had made a secret deal with Boabdil, son of Mulay Hassan and rival to the Arab throne held by his uncle Abdullah el Zagal, who had taken the throne when his brother Abul Hassan had become too old to rule effectively. Whilst Ferdinand plotted and schemed to defeat the enemy, Isabella raised the money for the campaign and inspired the troops. Mounted on her lively stallion, with her flashing green eyes and flowing chestnut hair, she led the columns and claimed the allegiance of her troops.

Jorge had outlined his plan to the men of the pueblo gathered in front of him, far up the slope of the hill above the village. Despite the limp that was the result of his injury in battle, he was an inspiring figure and speaker, and had long enthralled the youth of the village with his tales of Isabella leading the troops into battle. There had been many objections from some of the assembled villagers. "There are many more of them than us," said one; "they are better armed," chimed in another; "what if they are not fooled by the plan?" asked yet another; "if we wait, the army will arrive," was another objection. But surprisingly the old Comte had been firm in his support for the plan. He had been humiliated once too often by the Mudir of late, and had seen his limited authority taken away by the Moorish ruler. The Comte's one concern was for the Moors who were friendly to the Christians, especially those who had lived in the pueblo for years in

73

peace and harmony. He especially wanted no harm to come to Jalal, the grandson of Ali- Tūman, the old Mudir, or any of his family. The Comte insisted that they must be protected, and all other friendly Moors, especially those of Berber stock.

In the end, it was the young priest who had been sent secretly to the village to replace the one executed by the Moors who prevailed. This new priest was young and a rabid anti-Moor. A pupil of Fray Juan Pérez, the Queen's former confessor, he was active in the newly created Inquisition. He was at the time living in the village, masquerading as a labourer whilst also secretly performing the sacraments. "It's a good plan, drive them out of the village, with God's help you will prevail," was his judgement. And so it was agreed.

Two nights later, on a dark moonless night, the false rumour of the advance of a Christian force from the west had been spread through the Moorish *barrio* of the village. Aben Guzman gathered his men on the lower slopes of the *Collado de la Monticara,* the wild hill, one of the ridges that run north to south just outside the pueblo, on the route from the nearby village of Canillas, from where the supposed advance was coming.

Above them on the crest of the ridge a few women, some of the older children and some old men had been placed by Jorge, together with a large flock of goats with lanterns tied to their horns. When it became dark the lanterns were lit, and the animals were then driven down the steep hillside by the Christians towards the Moorish troops below. The women, children and old men shouted and called out slogans as they drove the goats down the hill, to simulate a large force of soldiers. At the same time, a handful of bowmen stationed further up the ridge fired off flight after flight of arrows as fast as they could.

The Moors below, under the impression that they had been outflanked by and were under attack from a large Spanish force, fled as best they could down the steep hillside, and along the side of the stream that ran through the steep-sided narrow valley at the bottom, to escape the attack.

Here, just above their route, on both sides of the stream, Jorge Ignacio had grouped the main body of his men. As the Moors stumbled in panic past them, they rained down a continuous shower of spears, darts, arrows and stones, and then they charged down upon the survivors and slew them with their swords, axes and knives. The Moors were killed almost to a man, the small stream running red with their blood. Ever since this time, the stream has been known as the *Río de Matanza,* or river of the slayings.

In the morning, the small victorious Christian band took possession of the Moorish hill fort, and gave the remaining Moors the choice of either leaving the village or staying as *Mudexares,* Moslem vassals. Many Moorish families stayed in the village, with a large percentage later converting to Christianity when the Moslems were finally made to return to Africa.

Shortly after this local battle, the news came to the pueblo of the capture of Vélez-Málaga by Isabella and Ferdinand, followed by the surrender of Bentomiz, Comares and other fortresses of the Axarquía.

Rumour of the battle in the pueblo, and the victory on the banks of the *Río de Matanza*, had been brought to Isabella as she journeyed through the Axarquía to join Ferdinand, who had moved on and was now besieging Málaga itself.

It was to Vélez-Málaga, whilst Isabella was resting there on her journey to Málaga, that Jorge Ignacio himself came, to bring the official news of the battle, victory and freeing of the pueblo, to his Queen.

After listening to his account of the affair, Isabella replied: *"Sé de ella"* or "I know of this".

Since that time, the pueblo has carried the name 'Sedella'.

CHAPTER 9

CARTAS DESDE SEDELLA
(Letters to and from Sedella)

In 1748, a boy was born in Sedella who was, when he grew up, to become a Capuchin monk and travel to Louisiana in the Americas as a missionary. He became a well loved figure there, and was remembered long after his death. Some of his exploits and the wider events that took place around him are set out here in a fictitious set of letters to a sister I have invented to be his correspondent in the village, together with other relevant documents. He was never to return to his birthplace. Records in Louisiana found some years ago, however, show that he was a well loved and respected man and remembered for his work locally, especially amongst the sick and the slaves of the region.

◊   ◊   ◊   ◊   ◊

Extract from a letter from the Bishop of Málaga to the Mayor of New Orleans, Louisiana, U.S.A. in February 1890:

.... with respect to your request for information about the life of Brother Antonio, a Capuchin of the Franciscan order, I enclose copies of papers collected by our archivist from our records that refer to him. Fray Antonio was born in 1748 in the village of Sedella, some distance from Málaga in the region of the Axarquía. He died, as you will be aware, in the Capuchin monastery near New Orleans in 1829, at the age of 81, having been active as a missionary in Louisiana for nearly 50 years until his retirement in 1821, due to his age and failing health. For much of his time in America, he corresponded with his younger sister Encarnación, and copies of such letters between them which remain are included with this letter. You have been kind enough to say that Fray Antonio is still remembered with affection in New Orleans, a comment which pleases me greatly. I am afraid to say that no-one in Málaga has any recollection of him, but perhaps this is understandable as he left here in 1773 to travel to the New World via

76

Cádiz. I have been told by the priest in Sedella, however, that his family there still speak of his exploits........

Note from the village priest of Sedella, Joseph Ximénez de Luna, to the Capuchin seminary in Malaga:

Sedella, August 1768

Your Honour,

This letter introduces Antonio who wishes to enter your seminary, with a view to joining the Capuchin order, and thereafter follow the life of a missionary in the Americas. He is of a good and God-fearing family, his father being a brother to our *alcalde,* mayor, Don Francisco Conde, and his mother a sister to Juan Andrés, the village miller and baker. He was born in the year of Our Lord 1748, and baptised by myself thereafter. Antonio took his first communion at the age of twelve, and served as an altar boy for many years. He is fully literate, can recite his creeds, knows the New Testament tolerably well and is numerate. His family back him fully in his calling to the life of a brother, his younger sister Encarnación, to whom he is very close, especially blesses this venture. I myself have no doubts as to his sincerity and calling, and can recommend his acceptance into the seminary.

I am Joseph Ximénez de Luna, Parish Priest of Sedella.

Capuchin Seminary, Málaga
July 1772

Joseph Ximénez de Luna,
Parish Priest
Esteemed Colleague,

The principal of the Seminary has instructed me to inform you that Fray Antonio, a member of your parish, took his final vows as a Franciscan brother of the Capuchin Order ten days ago. Following his wishes he has, with the approval of his superior, been put at the disposal of the Bishop of Cádiz, who is planning to send a group of missionaries to the New World next spring. He will initially travel to Vera Cruz, and from there be conveyed to New Orleans in the Viceroyalty of New Spain. The mission station to which he is going is near New Orleans, on the banks of the Mississippi river, and ministers to the ex-slaves, native Indians and both French and Spanish settlers.

I am, Fray Blas, secretary to the principal.

Captain Juan Carlos Cabeza y Ramos

Barco de Vela 'Gabriel'

Cádiz

April 1773

The Bishop of Cadiz,

Your Excellency,

I have today received on board ship six Franciscan brothers for passage to Vera Cruz in the Viceroyalty of New Spain, together with their luggage and sufficient ducats to cover the cost of their passage. Pray for our journey and that we do not fall prey to either storms or British privateers.

Your servant,

Juan Carlos, Captain.

Cartagena

Viceroyalty of New Granada

June 1773

Dearest Sister,

I write to tell you that we have arrived safely in the New World, not in New Spain as intended but in New Granada, many leagues to the south. Our journey that should have taken about a month has in the end lasted for nearer two. We left Cádiz, along with three other vessels, late in April, after celebrating Easter in the cathedral there. At first all went well, and then halfway across the Atlantic the trade winds which were in our favour died down and we were becalmed for about ten days. During this time, we saw many strange sea creatures which the sailors called Whales and Dolphins. When we were nearing the islands of Cuba and Hispaniola, where the great Cristóbal Colón first landed, we had to turn southwards to avoid a tropical storm centred on Martinique, which was barring our entrance into the Gulf of Mexico. So far south were we pushed, and so delayed had been our journey that the Captain, fearing we would run out of stores, finally put into port here in Cartagena. We now await a boat to take us to Vera Cruz where I, who am due to travel even further north to New Orleans, will have to embark on yet another ship. You would wonder at the countryside here which is wild and forested right down to the very shore, with tall trees and dense undergrowth, with such colourful flowers and birds, and lively animals in the trees called monkeys. It is hot, much hotter even than at home, and wet, every day rainstorms fill the air and afterwards the atmosphere is extremely humid. The local Indians go everywhere semi-naked, but as they are mostly primitives it is not considered sinful. Please pass on my love to our dear parents and all the family. If you write to me, and I pray you will, send the letter to the mission in New Orleans, as by that time I should have arrived there, God willing.

Your loving brother,
Antonio.

Sedella
Christmas 1773

Dearest Brother,

Your letter came as a joy to all the family, arriving as it did in November, and prior to the celebrations of the birth of our Saviour. Everyone in the pueblo sends you their love and blessings, and their hope that you have arrived safely at New Orleans after all your tribulations, how far away that seems to us here in the safety of the Axarquía. Our King, Carlos III, has introduced a new draft whereby one young man in five has to serve in the army for eight years, and Salvador Castro and Francisco Moreno, who you will remember as children, have already been conscripted. Several more from the pueblo have emigrated to the Americas, perhaps you may meet some of them, and one has returned after thirty years living near a town called Buenos Aires, on the *Río de la Plata*. I was very excited when he told me this, as I thought it may be close to where you are going. He told me however that it was far to the south of New Orleans, which he said was in French territory. This has puzzled me greatly, for I thought you were going to New Spain. He also said that Buenos Aires was more than three times more distant from New Orleans than we are from Paris in France. As I cannot comprehend that any country can be that big, I do not believe him, and am sure he is wrong on both counts. We all pray for your safety and look forward to another letter from you.

Your loving sister,

Encarnación.

Capuchin Monastery

New Orleans

December 1775

Dearest Sister,

Your letter of Christmas 1773 did not reach me until just over a month ago. I have so much to tell you. I arrived here in the August of 1773 nearly four months later than I was expected. New Orleans is on the banks of a large river, surrounded by swamp and jungle. Four days before we reached harbour, the sea was full of debris that had flowed down the river, and the water was no longer salty. The land is entirely flat, no hills whatsoever, not at all like at home. The river itself is brown and muddy with large creatures called alligators, which have jaws full of sharp teeth. Big snakes, some of which are said to be poisonous, also live in the water and the surrounding jungle. The town itself is mainly built out of wooden houses, and was only founded in 1718. It is a port, with boats coming and going both up and down the river and by sea to many destinations, including Cádiz. Our mission house is a short distance upstream from the town, and is best reached by boat from there. It is constructed from both timber and adobe, and is equipped with a fine bell. The reason that the man from Buenos Aires thought that New Orleans was French is that at one time it was. For many years apparently, so I have been told, both France and Spain claimed the land. The territory is even called Louisiana, after Louis IV of France. In the late 1600's Robert Cavalier, a Frenchman, finally won the argument and so it became French. However, twelve years ago Louis XV, the French King, gave the whole of Louisiana including New Orleans to his cousin Carlos, our own King. There are still many French settlers here as well as numerous Spanish ones, many from around Málaga. There are some native Indians nearby, but most of these are found further up river, and on the vast plains to the north and east of here. The majority of the population are black Africans who were slaves, but who were freed about forty years ago by the French rulers. Most of our missionary work is with these ex-slaves who work on the farms producing cotton, maize and sugar. Nearer the town most of the work is in the forests, cutting down the trees and planting up the new cleared land. One of the reasons why I had not read your letter earlier is that I have been on a long journey to a mission station many leagues to the west, as far as the vast plains of Texas. Here the main occupation is rearing cattle, and I saw some of the giant buffaloes that roam there. These are huge cattle, bigger than our Andalucían bulls, with large horns and thick hairy necks. The local Indians hunt them for meat and use their skins for many purposes. When I returned to New Orleans, the town was alive with rumours of a war in the British territories to the north, where the settlers are fighting for independence. Please pass on my love to all the family, and my regards to all those in the pueblo who still remember me.

Your loving brother,

Antonio.

Extract from a communiqué from the Prior of the Capuchin settlement in New Orleans to the Abbot of the father house in Málaga 1783:

...................We were much disturbed in the last three years by the war in the British territories to the north. Soldiers from the armies of Holland, France and Spain, who were engaged in helping the new American states against the British, passed through the city frequently. There was much fighting further up the Mississippi where the British were claiming Louisiana for their crown, and we were inundated with the wounded of all nations. Brother Antonio from your house was put in charge of the hospital we opened to tend these injured men, and carried out his task with great skill. He has turned out to be a very reliable brother and is looked up to by all the populace of the city, where he is well known for his missionary zeal and his practical help to the poor and needy.........

Dearest Sister,

Your letters telling of the peaceful nature of life in the pueblo always fill me with pleasure. Your life, since your marriage to José and the death of our dear parents, must be very different from the one I remember. It is certainly a contrast to the one I live here, which is in constant turmoil. You will remember I wrote to you in 1801 explaining that a new Governor, Manuel Juan de Salcerdo, had arrived from Spain. What nobody knew at that time, not even the new Governor, was that Godoy, on behalf of our King Carlos, at the Treaty of San Idefonso in 1800, had already given Louisiana back to Napoleon Bonaparte of France. Then two years ago, after the signing of the peace treaty at Amiens between France and Britain, we had an influx of new settlers from England and Scotland. At about this time, Napoleon sent Pierre Clément de Laussat as his ambassador to take possession of the state for France. Of course, no-one here knew that the land had been given back to France, and when he realised what was happening Rigo, one of the local Spanish generals, tried to set up an independent state with himself at its head. The general confusion was made worse when Toussinaint, a French general, tried to do the same thing. This was compounded by Napoleon sending at the same time a decree rescinding the freedom of the ex-slaves, and the French army started to take them back into custody. This action brought about a rebellion of the blacks, and our ports were blockaded by the French and Spanish navies. Worse was to come, as during this same time there was an outbreak of smallpox, which was very bad indeed amongst the black community. I was put in charge of the mission hospital once again and was very busy indeed. The whole area was full of fighting between the blacks, the British, French and Spanish settlers, and the Spanish and French armies, and we also had to care for many wounded. Then, just a few months ago, Napoleon sold Louisiana to the new United States of America, without telling his representative Laussat what he had done. Since then the American President, Jefferson, has invaded all the land with his troops, and is slowly restoring peace and order. I am afraid however that the poor blacks are the losers for, after being smitten with the smallpox, crippled by the blockade and killed by the forces of Britain, France and our own Spain, the Americans have now taken them all back into slavery. Pray for them and for me, dear sister.

Your loving brother,
Antonio.

Sedella

Christmas 1805

Dearest Antonio,

I am writing this letter to you, once more at Christmas, with a sense of anxiety as I have not received one from you for over two years and I am concerned for your safety. I tell myself that it is the recent war with Britain that has stopped their arrival, but this thought brings me little comfort. The children and José all send their love, as do all the rest of the family, all your brothers and sisters and now numerous nephews and nieces. We have had an exciting if turbulent year during the time of the conflict. From the village, we could often see the British ships off the shores below as they patrolled to and fro, and many men of the pueblo have been away fighting, some never to return, I fear. And then, just over a month ago, we heard news of the big sea battle near Cádiz at Cabo de Trafalgar, where the British fleet destroyed ours. Many French and Spanish ships were sunk, and it is rumoured that the British Admiral was killed at his moment of triumph. This disaster has at least ended the war, and I may look forward once again to news of you, good news I pray.

Your loving sister,
Encarnación.

Vélez-Málaga

Easter 1806

Dearest Antonio,

I write this short letter to you with great joy. Your letter of January 1804 has just arrived here. It has been long delayed by the war, as I had hoped and prayed was the case. We have suffered an unusually wet winter, but all the farmers say that this will be good for the *campo* and the crops. This year we had a special treat, as we have travelled down to Vélez to stay with *Tío Pepe,* Uncle Joseph, who now lives here and sends you his love, he says he stills laughs when he remembers the first time you tried to ride his mule when you were a boy, and kept falling off time and time again. On Good Friday, we watched the *Cofradías* parade; the *Real Cofradía del Santo Sepulcro* was splendid indeed. On Sunday, yesterday, we went to a mass in the church of San Juan. I give thanks to God that you are still in good health.

Your loving sister,

Encarnación.

Note from the archivist to the Bishop of Málaga to the Mayor of New Orleans, inserted into the file of letters between brother and sister:

These are all the letters that remain for the time up to 1806, there are obviously several gaps in their sequence. From 1806 we have unfortunately only two more in our possession. There was understandably a gap in the correspondence in any case, due to the renewed war between France and the combined glorious allies of Spain, Portugal and Great Britain which, as you will be aware, did not finally end until 1814. Our records of Fray Antonio are compiled from his personal effects which were brought back to Málaga from New Orleans after his death in 1829, together with letters kept by his sister, Encarnación, forwarded to us by the parish priest of Sedella when she died in 1831; her family thought that they may have been of interest to us. The missing ones have either been mislaid or destroyed, but I trust that the enclosed ones will enable you to form a picture of his life and character. The Bishop is anxious to accede to your request to the very best of our ability, and I will be very glad to answer any questions you might have on the matter. The remaining two letters follow. I am your humble servant,

(Signature illegible).

Dearest Sister,

I am writing another letter to you in the hope that it will reach you safely, as by now the news here is that Napoleon's army has been vanquished from Andalucía, and is retreating from the whole of the country. I pray that both you and all our family have come safely through the war, and are in good health and spirits. I have little hope that the letters I wrote to you during the conflict have found their way to my village in the hills. O how I miss the landscape and people of my youth. At times I grow weary of the flatness and marshy jungle land that surrounds us here, and in the type of society that exists in the nearby city of New Orleans where I spend so much of my time. It has to be said that whilst the new American rulers have brought order and stability to the region, there is a laxity in the morals of the town, and the state of the slaves is pitiable. But it is God's will that I am here and I must not complain, even if I long sometimes for the pueblo of my youth. Write and tell me all is well. Today, the day of the Ascension of our blessed Lord Jesus, has been a busy one for me as you may imagine. As well as my work in the mission hospital where I now spend much time, the brothers have had celebrations and masses to fit the occasion. It is now quite late at night, and I am relaxing before sleep by writing to you and thinking of your life. Whilst the State of Louisiana, which is what the Americans call this area, is now free of conflict, the remaining Spanish possessions here are in constant turmoil. Many of the districts of the vast southern continent have of recent years been demanding their independence from the homeland. Francisco de Miranda, a rebel leader in that land, is waging such a war and calling his new proposed land, which he wants to encompass all that continent bar that owned by Portugal, Columbia. You may not be able to comprehend the size of this southern continent, but it is many times the size of the whole of Europe. Even here in the Viceroyalty of New Spain, of which we were once a part, there is trouble, this time led, if we can believe the rumours, by two priests! God forbid it is so. What is true is that these revolutions are fostered by the *Criollos,* Creoles. These Criollos are either people of pure Spanish blood, or of a mixture of Spanish and native Indian or black blood. God help us all for the future.

Your loving brother,

Antonio.

Sedella

Christmas 1813

Dearest Antonio,

It was very good to get your recent letter, but I grieve at your longing for home and wish every day that we will meet again some time, but fear that your calling and the vast distance that separates us will not allow this. My news to you is both good but also sad. We were under French rule for over two years, with their troops stationed at Vélez-Málaga and even in Canillas de Aceituno. You will have heard of the dreadful tidings from Madrid in May of 1808, when many were massacred and the war began. Our own government was under siege in Cádiz for over two years, but a Spanish army was active nearby during nearly all of this time led by General Ballesteros, he even seized and held Málaga for a short while. In the pueblo, we had our own small guerrilla force, which proved very troublesome to the French army. You will remember Antonio Negro, you were children together, well his son Antonio Negrito was their leader and was just known by his nickname of El Negrito. This was so that the French would not know who he was. In August last year, when the French were retreating, a force from Alcaucín was in conflict with Negrito's men, together with some of Ballesteros' troops. They engaged in a battle just outside the village where the track comes up from Valverde. Our side won the engagement but there were heavy losses on both sides, including my own dear son Manuel and two of our nephews. So whereas we are now free of the dreadful French, my own loss is very deep. I cannot tell you how much I look forward to having letters from you, and hearing of your life in the States of America which is so different from my own. Another sadness is that my José has not been in good health of late, with aches and pains which are much worse in the damp and cold periods. At present the days are fine and even warm in the sun, and so he is much easier. Write and tell me more of the strange land where you dwell.

Your loving sister,
Encarnación.

CHAPTER 10

LA GUERRA DE LA INDEPENDENCIA
(The Peninsular War)

The history of *La Guerra de la Independencia,* the War of Independence, as the Spanish call this period, or the Peninsular War as it is more commonly called by the British, is well recorded. However, a short resume of the position both nationally and in the pueblo of Sedella is worth giving.

In 1808, Napoleon seized Spain and so ended his alliance with that country. He 'kidnapped' the Spanish Bourbon king and replaced him with his, Napoleon's, own elder brother, Joseph Bonaparte. Spain had until then been his ally in the war against the British, but eventually became his foe allied with them. On the second of May 1808, the populace of Madrid rose up against the French, being in turn crushed by the French on the following day.

Napoleon had already packed northern Spain with his troops in readiness to invade Portugal. The French army was made up not only of Frenchmen, but also French North Africans, Italians, Dutchmen, Germans, Austrians and many more nationalities who were in free or forced allegiance with France.

First Moore and later, after his death, Wellington defended Portugal against the French forces, carrying the battle to and fro across that country and Spain in the five year campaign. During the whole of the Peninsular War the English, Portuguese and Spanish regular troops numbered but a fraction of the French forces arrayed against them. However, despite this they were able to hold their own and eventually triumph. Wellington was an able general but the French had their own leaders who were his equal, including Napoleon himself. To understand the reason for the British success, the nature of the war must be understood. There were two factors of great import that added to Wellington's superiority and eventual victory.

The first factor was the British Navy who controlled the seas, blockading the French fleet in harbour, and ensuring that all supplies to the French army had to be brought into and through Spain by land, travelling through hostile country and having to pass through wild mountain ranges and arid plains down the length of that country. The navy also patrolled the Spanish coastline and heavily bombarded any column of troops attempting to travel along the coastal strip, forcing them inland. They also had orders to liaise with the Spanish army and guerrillas, giving them aid in the nature of guns, powder, shot and even money wherever practical. The navy in return accepted French prisoners of war, conveying them to the prison hulks at Gibraltar and elsewhere.

The second factor was the Spanish army and the irregulars who defended their country. Ignored and much maligned by most British commentators they were, arguably, the most important factor in Napoleon's defeat and Wellington's victory.

The Spanish army, as well as fighting alongside Wellington, also operated on Spanish soil in their own right. They fought in many places before being mainly contained in 1810 by Soult's army around Cádiz. The guerrillas operated all over Spain in mountainous regions throughout the whole of the war. Their actions tied up the French army everywhere in Spain, and garrisons were needed across the whole country to both keep open the supply lines and maintain order. Therefore, whilst the total French army of occupation may have been four of five times that of Wellington's, only a fraction of them could be deployed in the field to face him. The guerrillas, it is estimated, killed more of the French troops over the course of the war than did Wellington's more conventional army, with relatively small losses themselves.

There were many famous Spanish guerrilla leaders notably Juan Martín Díaz, 'El Empecinado' (the stubborn); the priest Merino; Sarasa 'Cholin'; Porlier 'El Marquesito' (the little Marques); and perhaps most famous of all, Mina el Mozo 'El Estudiante' (the student), and his uncle Espoz y Mina, who both operated in the Asturias.

Most of the leaders were known by nicknames as in many parts of the country they lived ordinary lives, working the fields and going about their normal business most days and then, at other times, taking part in guerrilla activities, returning every night to their homes.

The whole population, men, women and children, were united in opposing the army of occupation. There is a story of a boy of about 8 living near Ronda who led a party of Hussars into an ambush, whilst pretending to guide them through the countryside. In the evenings, when the French forces stationed in the many small forts around the country returned from patrol and darkness fell, they could hear all round them the songs and taunts of the guerrillas from the surrounding towns. The local Spanish also fed well whilst hiding their stores from the French, who relied on local produce to live. Likewise, the Spanish regular army could vanish into the countryside after a battle, to reform some time and distance away.

It was this total opposition by all the populace that tied up so many of the French troops, paralysed their mobility, and reduced their ability to concentrate on fighting the forces of Wellington.

Guerrilla warfare was born in Spain, the very word 'guerrilla' being the Spanish for 'little war'. Then and since, this form of warfare has shown the impossibility of an invading army subduing a total population. By 1810 Andalucía, with the exception of Cádiz, was under French control. However, during the two years of its subjugation to French rule, Málaga was once re-taken for a while by the Spanish army, and General Ballesteros was active in the countryside throughout the occupation. The mountains around Ronda and Málaga, together with the Axarquía and the Alpujarras, were also alive with Spanish guerrilla and irregular forces.

In August 1812, General Soult, the French commander of the armies of occupation of Andalucía, decided to withdraw from the province and retreat to Madrid. Soult was prompted in this by Wellington's consolidation of his hold on Portugal, and subsequent advance from here on to the Spanish capital. Soult had long refused to move out of Andalucía and join the French forces fighting Wellington further north in Spain and Portugal. Indeed, he had been unable to do so by the need to continue the siege of Cádiz, seat of the Spanish government, contain the guerrillas and mobilise against the Spanish general Ballesteros, whose forces were active in the province of Andalucía. By August however, Soult faced being cut off and isolated from the main French forces to the north and from France itself by the actions of the combined armies of England, Spain and Portugal moving across Extremadura towards Madrid. For the same reason, he could not retreat directly north, and so he decided to go first eastwards towards Granada, and then turn north towards Valencia. Abandoning the siege of Cádiz, he withdrew eastwards together with his forces based at Sevilla, Ronda and Málaga and the many smaller bases throughout the area.

History records a battle taking place near *loma parra* just outside Sedella between the retreating French forces, and the guerrillas of the pueblo (said to be one of the biggest in the area) and a detachment of Ballesteros' army.

◊　◊　◊　◊　◊

The order to withdraw reached the small garrison in Alcaucín in the Axarquía towards the end of August, delayed inevitably for well over a week because of the action of the guerrillas of the Montes de Málaga. Major Henri Le Brun, commander of the garrison, read the message with mounting consternation and dismay. His force occupied what had been an old Moorish hill fort that he had partly rebuilt, roofed and fortified. His task was to keep open one of the main routes through the sierras from Córdoba in the north to the coast, for the movement of men and materials. This route passed close to Alcaucín on its descent from the pass of Zafarraya, above the town, to Vélez-Málaga near the coast below. This route had long been of strategic importance and as such had featured in many past struggles, and would do so again in future times.

Because his orders had been so long delayed, he now knew the reason why the Spanish colours had been viewed flying at the top of the pass at Zafarraya. The French forces from Ronda and Antequera had been passing the head of the pass whilst retreating over the *vega* beyond the sierras, towards Alhama de Granada, closely followed by the advancing Spanish and English forces in their wake. This route of escape was therefore no longer open to him. In addition, as he looked down towards the distant coastline, he could make out the long columns of the French army retreating from Málaga, closely followed

91

by their pursuers. It would not therefore be possible to descend to Vélez and retreat along the coastline, the easiest route to the east. Indeed, a small group of French Hussars had already arrived at Alcaucín shortly after the orders to retreat, having fled from Vélez which they reported as already in Spanish hands.

Major Le Brun therefore considered his options. Both the routes eastwards to the north over the flat *vegas,* and to the south along the coast, were cut off from him. The only alternative was to make his way by the much more difficult route along the foothills of the Sierras de Tejeda and Almijara.

This route would take him by mule tracks along the line of the sierras where the first steep slopes levelled out, before falling more gradually to the coast below. He would then be able to turn north towards Granada by way of either of the passes from Almuñecar or Motril. This would be a difficult trek, the tracks tortuously twisting and turning, and dropping in and out of steep-sided valleys, prone to attack from guerrillas all along its route. He was however a brave and determined officer, and not given to vacillation. The choice was either to attempt this route, or surrender to the allied forces that would soon be moving towards him from both north and south.

His small force of men was therefore made ready to abandon their fortress, together with a pack train of mules, the following morning. Their route would take them through the Axarquía by way of Canillas de Aceituno, where they would be augmented by the small outpost of some twenty Austrian mountain guards who held that post for the Napoleonic cause. From Canillas, his plan was to travel past Sedella, Salares, Árchez and Cómpeta, before turning and dropping below the crest of the Sierra de Almijara, until the coast was reached somewhere to the east of Nerja. The most dangerous part of the route, he knew, would be near Sedella and Salares, where the Spanish irregular forces were most active.

That same evening, news of the pending retreat reached Rodrigo Antonio Górriz, known by the name of 'El Negrito', the leader of the Sedella guerrillas, as he worked in his vineyard, the harvest being nearly due. All the country were part of the resistance to the forces of occupation, and the inhabitants of Alcaucín heard of the proposed orders to withdraw almost as soon as Le Brun issued them, and despatched a fleet-footed youth to Sedella at once. El Negrito paused in his work and sent one of his sons who was working with him into the pueblo to rouse the rest of his men, and another to Vélez to inform the newly arrived Spanish army of the situation.

Rodrigo Antonio Górriz, 'El Negrito', formed his band of guerrillas in the pueblo shortly after the fall of Andalucía in 1810. Locally, the town of Vélez-Málaga had a large French garrison, whilst many other smaller towns, such as Alcaucín, also had French forces billeted in them.

El Negrito was able to carry out a campaign of harassing the forces at Canillas, some 7 km away; going over the sierra and descending on to the *vega* around Alhama to attack the supply trains moving across it between Granada and Antequera; and also attacking the supply route between Zafarraya and Vélez.

The biggest problem he had, however, was in obtaining arms and ammunition. When he had formed his group, it had only had a few old carbines and some ancient swords and spears. Over time, he managed to augment these with muskets, pikes, swords and the like captured from the enemy. However, powder and shot were always a problem, and more arms were always needed. After one successful foray, he had taken four Italian prisoners and, hearing of the British Navy's policy of exchanging prisoners for supplies, devised a plan to acquire more guns and munitions. El Negrito and a small band of his men had therefore travelled down from Sedella to the coast, avoiding the shoreline just below Vélez where the French force occupied an ancient tower from Moorish times, *'El Torre del Mar'*. They had reached the coast at the small fishing village of Lagos, where they persuaded the local fishermen to lend them a boat, and had headed out towards a British frigate on patrol offshore.

Captain James Frobisher, commander of His Britannic Majesty's frigate Pericles, was bored. Sitting in his small cabin, he had been engaged in writing to his wife. This letter had been started two weeks ago and added to each day, and would continue to be added to until a supply boat arrived to carry it off. And what to say that had not already been said many times? The frigate was engaged in the blockade of the Spanish coastline, its beat being from Málaga in the west to Motril in the east, back and forth, for weeks on end. Even the weather, in these balmy Mediterranean days of early summer, had remained calm and fine, so that there were no high winds or seas to contend with. The frigate simply went westwards using the light levante winds, and then reached back eastwards in three or four long tacks.

Captain Frobisher's mind had wandered away in a daydream. His eyes gazed out of the stern windows at the coast on the horizon. He thought of the fragrant oil of the olives, the fresh meat, vegetables and fruit just a few miles away. His mind turned to the sweet Málaga wine produced nearby, just a few leagues distance across the clear blue of the Mediterranean. His own stores of fresh food were by now long gone and his last butter had been eaten, rancid, from the stone crock weeks ago. Shipboard fare consisted only of hard ship's biscuit, salt pork and beef, dried beans and lentils, and some, by now, half-rotten root vegetables. And so near, yet so far, fresh food that at least would relieve the monotony of the blockade duties.

The captain's reverie had been broken by rapid footsteps outside his cabin, and the entry of George Taylor, at just 16 the youngest midshipman aboard the frigate.

"Mr Gray's compliments, sir," piped the youngster, "but there's a boat pulling out from the shore towards us."

The captain rose, pulling on his uniform coat and clapping his cocked hat onto his head.

"Very well, Mr Taylor, tell the first lieutenant I'm coming up at once," the captain replied. "And pass the word for my secretary, Mr Delgado, to join me there."

"Aye aye, sir," the midshipman replied, and disappeared from view at a run.

Reaching the deck, the captain had glanced quickly around the ship to check that all was well, and then joined his officers who were grouped together viewing the approaching boat.

"Begging your pardon, sir," said the first lieutenant, "but them's Italian soldiers by the look of 'em in the bow. Shall I warn 'em off?"

"Four soldiers would never attempt to attack a frigate, Mr Gray," replied the captain with a smile. "And look, they're under guard from the others in the boat - ah, Mr Delgado," he continued to his secretary, who had just arrived. "Ask 'em who they are, if you please."

Eduardo Delgado, the captain's secretary, was of Spanish and English parentage and had been employed by one of the sherry houses in Jerez until hostilities had halted the trade. He was now enrolled in His Britannic Majesty's Navy as a secretary, and employed in the blockade as a Spanish speaker.

"It's a local guerrilla leader and some of his men, with captives taken in a skirmish against a supply train - their leader's one El Negrito, the local commander," he had reported after a brief shouted conversation with the nearing boat.

"Turn out the marine guard," ordered the captain to his first lieutenant. "Invite 'em aboard, Mr Delgado, if you please. Now, Sergeant Giles," he continued to the marine sergeant. "Pipe up the Spanish as they come aboard."

So it was that El Negrito of Sedella and his men had been piped aboard the British frigate by two marine privates. He looked keenly about him at the strange spectacle afforded by a British man of war, and had soon been shaking hands with Captain Frobisher.

Delgado had quickly established that the Spanish had brought prisoners and requested in return muskets, powder and shot, and perhaps some gold to help their cause. The captain had quickly agreed to supply twenty muskets and a quantity of powder and shot, twenty cutlasses, and some gold coins he had captured off a French privateer some time ago. Over a glass of rum, much appreciated by the Spaniards, he had outlined a plan that was rapidly being formulated in his mind.

"Perhaps you could take a few of my men, say two sailors and two marines under a midshipman, back to your village, what was its name again? Ah yes, Sedella, thank you kindly Mr Delgado, to Sedella then and allow them to purchase some bread, olive oil, some vegetables and perhaps oranges. And meat, what meat have you? What's that? Pork, goat, rabbit and chicken, admirable and perhaps a few eggs, and some goat's milk? Splendid. Now, some of your local sweet wine and a bottle or two of the local brandy? I'll pay handsomely for it all, and I'll hire a couple of mules to bring it all back to the shore."

The captain had been in his element, helping the guerrillas as orders laid down, by supplying arms, taking charge of prisoners also as ordered, and stocking his own and the wardroom's store with fresh food.

Both sides were equally pleased with the arrangements made, and soon the boat had been heading back to shore with five British men replacing the four Italian soldiers in the bows. It was in this way that five Britons, three sailors and two marines, had come to stay in Sedella for a few days during the first week of June 1810. One of the sailors, a fiery red-haired Irishman, Martin O'Neil, being not too keen on the life at sea, having been pressed for service a few months previously, had gone missing and had to be left behind on their return. O'Neil had taken a fancy to a local black-haired Spanish señorita, whose family had hidden him away from all attempts by the rest of the shore party to find him.

This event established El Negrito as the main local guerrilla leader, and the pueblo of Sedella as the centre of the local irregular forces, as well as providing him with an able lieutenant in Martin O'Neil. Over the coming months, the guerrillas of Sedella carried out many raids, increasing in numbers and reputation. Between actions they returned home to continue work on their olives, grapes, almonds and other crops, in the way of all Spanish irregulars.

And now in August 1812, the end of the occupation of Andalucía was at hand with the French streaming in retreat towards Granada. On the morning after the news of the pending retreat of the garrison from Alcaucín, El Negrito formed his band of irregulars on a hillside just to the west of the pueblo at *La Portadilla,* the little door, in readiness to harass the retreating French forces. His total force was in the region of some fifty men, with a few boys and older men to augment this.

Le Brun's force numbered in total over 400, being his own garrison, the Hussars from Vélez, the garrison from Viñuela lower down the pass, and the Austrian mountain guards who they would join up with in Canillas.

In the early afternoon, this force was nearing the hidden Spanish irregulars, having passed through Canillas and then clambered up the steep hill towards *el puerto,* the pass, some way outside Sedella. When they reached the top of the winding climb up to Puerto, the French troops were hot and sweaty in the strong August sun which was already high in the sky. Whilst Le Brun rested his force after the climb, El Negrito, waiting about a kilometre away, saw a group of Spanish cavalry followed by a column of infantrymen approaching along a track which led from just outside Sedella, through the *aldea,* hamlet, of Valverde to Vélez. This force, part of the army of General Ballesteros, which had entered Vélez after the retreat of the French, had been dispatched early that morning in response to El Negrito's message of the previous evening.

Joining forces with the guerrillas, who came out of hiding to meet them, the combined force of cavalry, infantrymen, the local irregulars and two field pieces brought by the regular soldiers, formed up at the head of a small valley through which the track from Canillas ran. The ridge where the Spanish force waited was called *loma parra,* (and is still known by that name today) and it was situated above the *río de matanza*, site of an earlier battle between the Christian and Moorish forces during the re-conquest. A battle which led to Sedella getting its name.

Le Brun saw the Spanish troops drawn up, blocking his way, and decided to try and break through their line, a move that was necessary if he was not to turn back or surrender. Pushing out two groups of foot soldiers to attack either flank of the Spanish force and draw their fire, he then led the cavalry in a charge up to the main body of the defenders on the rise ahead.

The Spanish artillery cut a swathe through the charging Hussars and then their own cavalry, followed by some of the foot soldiers, counter attacked the French. The guerrillas meanwhile repulsed the French who were attacking the flanks.

The battle was brief, fierce and bloody, with many dead and wounded on both sides, before the French were eventually forced to yield and surrender. As the official account of the battle reads, 'the Spanish army triumphed, taking many French prisoners'.

97

This event was the end of *La Guerra de la Independencia* as far as Sedella was concerned.

A few weeks later, the whole of Andalucía was free of the French occupiers. In about another year, Spain itself was rid of Bonaparte's occupation, which ended at Molinos Del Rey on 10th January 1814, when Soult fought his last battle on Spanish soil before retreating to France.

In Sedella, Rodrigo Antonio Górriz returned to the life of an ordinary hill farmer. The Irishman, Martin O'Neil, lived on in the pueblo where he too became a peasant hill farmer, growing the local crops with the help of his family, after marrying his Spanish *novia*, Esperanza.

CHAPTER 11

LOS TRASTORNOS
(The disturbances)

On the 23rd of February 1886, a 'political argument and assault' occurred in the pueblo that resulted in the death of the ex-municipal judge, Francisco Aguilar. As a result of this, the *alcalde,* mayor, and several other persons were arrested for murder. The origins of these events dated back to the disturbances of nearly fifty years before. In 1842, a revolt took place in Sedella, and that revolt was itself related to earlier national problems. These had begun in the early 1840's, during the early days of the reign of the new Queen, Isabella ll.

She was only 10 when she first came to the throne, and was under the regency of General Baldomero Espartero. Her uncle, Don Carlos, her father's brother, claimed the throne in her place. Despite having just lost a civil war, his supporters were still agitating to bring Carlos to the throne. At the same time, many factions were arguing with the liberalising policies of Espartero's government. The growing number of anarchists and progressives were demanding more changes, whilst on the other hand the Church and the ultra conservatives opposed any change whatsoever. Even the moderates in the army were against Espartero.

These problems between the Queen and Carlos, and the deep divisions of the political parties of the left and right, and the Church, were to fester on for many years and erupt finally in the Civil War in 1936.

In Sedella, they were also at the root of the disturbances that ended with the murder of Don Aguilar.

◊　◊　◊　◊　◊

For three days, the lawyer sent from Málaga to represent the alcalde of Sedella and a few other officials of the council, all arrested on a charge of murder, had had his journey delayed at Vélez-Málaga. It was March of 1886, and the spring rains had poured down during the three days, making the roads impassable. The rains turned the tracks to mud and the gentle streams into roaring torrents. On the first day alone, more than 100 litres of water per square metre had fallen, according to the new measuring equipment in the town. Since then the downfall had eased, but by his reckoning over 200 mm of water had been deposited in total over the three days. On the fourth day the rain had ceased, the clouds lifted and the sun had shone. He decided that, if it remained dry, he would be able to continue his journey on the next day.

During the time he spent cooped up in the *posada*, waiting for the rain to stop, the lawyer, Ramon, had chatted to the young man Paco, the son of one of the accused, who had been sent from the village to Vélez to accompany him on the final stage of his journey. Paco had been given the task of explaining the events leading up to the murder, and fill in any local knowledge Ramon needed to supplement the official notes on the case.

Ramon, at twenty-six, was well educated, being a graduate of Madrid University, and was acquainted with the law as well as the history and politics of the time. Paco was the son of one of the small peasant farmers of the village, not yet twenty years old, and unable to either read or write. Both men however got on well together, and were soon friends as well as travelling companions.

Paco's initial explanation of the situation was simple. His father, he explained, together with the mayor and the others, had got into a heated argument with the murdered man, ex-municipal judge, Don Francisco Aguilar. The argument had been over one of Don Francisco's decisions, some years ago when he was still a judge, regarding some property that had belonged to the mayor's family. Or had not belonged to the mayor's family according to the then judge, who had ruled in favour of the other party to the dispute, who had been the *alcalde* at the time of the case. The quarrel had turned violent, and someone in the accused group had stabbed Don Francisco.

"It was done in heat," argued Paco. "It's simple, they argued, got passionate, Don Aguilar would not listen, he pushed and shouted, it was an accident."

Ramon knew it was far from simple, or rather it was simple, a quick spur of the moment flare of temper, but that it was rooted far back in the complexities of the past; made complicated beyond belief and almost beyond understanding in *los trastornos,* the disturbances, that had lasted for nearly fifty years. He was also aware that the start of the present day troubles, which ended in the murder of the ex-judge, lay in a revolt that had taken place in Sedella in 1842, forty-four years before, and that the revolt was itself related to events nationally.

The two men first examined what had happened at that time. Ramon began by explaining to the local youngster the situation that had existed in the early 1840's in Spain, during the early days of the new Queen, Isabella II.

Ramon outlined in great detail the political position prior to the *pronunciamientos,* military uprisings, that took place all over Andalucía in 1843, and which led to the eventual overthrow of General Espartero. Paco was well aware of the events in Sedella, which although happening before his birth were still the subject of local arguments. He explained to the lawyer what he knew of the events of that time.

"In the pueblo then, the priest and a local landowner, Don José Hurtado, both ultra conservatives, held the village tightly in control. Most of the locals were radicals, and in 1841 they elected a left wing mayor who tried to bring about changes. These changes Don José blocked and in the following year the village rose in revolt, in support of the mayor. During the revolt Don José was injured and the mayor, together with several others, was arrested." He paused and smiled at Ramon. "It must have been almost like what has just happened this year, except that Don José did not die, and the mayor and his supporters were soon released for lack of evidence."

Before they left Vélez to start the journey to Sedella on the following morning, the lawyer also learned from Paco that following his release from prison, and whilst Don José was still absent from the village in hospital, the mayor had annexed a piece of land belonging to the injured man.

"The land was really his anyway," claimed the young man. "Don José was holding it illegally in the first place. The mayor simply took it back and gave it to the legal owner," he affirmed.

The man he gave it back to was the mayor's own cousin, thought Ramon, who had background notes on the case. He did not voice his thoughts aloud though, simply observing that, "this land has been in dispute ever since then, hasn't it?" to which Paco agreed.

The two men made an early start the next morning, riding north out of Vélez through the cluster of small brick making works that lay beside the road. Smoke from the stacks of burning clay rose in the air around them as they passed by. The men working next to the clamps of bricks, pushing soft clay into wooden trays, paused to watch the pair of riders go by.

During the morning, Ramon outlined the growing national problems in the years between the revolt and the murder in Sedella. In this period three generals, Ramon María Narváez, Francisco Serrano and Leopoldo O'Donnell, vied with each other as head of state. O'Donnell, despite his Irish name, was in fact a Spaniard. The frequent changes of rule between the three men was one of the factors which contributed to the continual lack of stability in the country. Another factor that added to the national turmoil was the behaviour of the young Queen. Isabella was a good looking and buxom young girl, but she was unfortunately also passionate and promiscuous. During her short reign, she took many lovers (including General Serrano), a practice that did not cease after her marriage, at 16, to her effeminate cousin Francisco de Asis. Also during this time, the Carlist faction kept up their agitation forcing the country into a second civil war in their pursuit of the throne for Don Carlos.

Finally, Ramon explained, in 1868 a fourth general, Juan Prim, made his *pronunciamiento* and became head of state. He deposed Isabella, sending her into exile, and put Amadeo, the Duke of Aosta in Italy, in her place. Unfortunately, Prim was assassinated and Aosta rejected by the whole country. These two events were followed by a coup, which overthrew the monarchy and established a Republic in 1873.

Paco, in his turn, explained to the lawyer that during this turbulent period nationally, in the village the two groupings of radicals and conservatives had maintained and strengthened their positions. Locally, the dispute between them revolved around parochial rather than national issues. The parties referred to themselves not as conservatives or radicals, but as 'us' and 'them'. Whilst the leaders of the two factions were linked to, and supported, the respective national parties, the villagers simply followed where they led. The biggest group in the pueblo had been and still was, he stated, to the left politically and had welcomed the forming of the first Republic.

When questioned by the lawyer about the land that had been in dispute, Paco answered that he thought its significance had faded over the years; it had become a token of the problem rather than the problem itself. Even the exact boundaries of the plot of land in question were now unclear.

Some way out of the town, the two men paused in their journey on the crest of the first rise, to rest their horses. Behind them was the coastal plain with the town of Vélez in the foreground, the old Moorish fort towering high above it. Beyond the town, the waters of the sea were a deep blue merging into a grey haze on the horizon. In front of them, the ground fell away to rise again to another ridge that stood between them and Sedella.

When they began their journey once more, Ramon took up his story again. "The Republic lasted barely a year," he began. "It was then overthrown by another general, Martínez Campos, who restored the monarchy. The new King was Alfonso XII, who is still our King now. At the time General Campos put him on the throne, he was only 16 years old and was in England at their army school of Sandhurst. During the time Campos was in office, the army finally defeated the Carlists to end a third attempt by them to put Don Carlos María, a descendant of the original pretender, on to the throne. Soon after that the army handed power back to the civilians, just ten years ago, when Antonio Cánovas brought in the new constitution."

At this point, Paco broke in on the lawyer's explanation. "Ah yes, Cánovas!" he said. "The 'monster' from Málaga. He's the leader of 'them', the right, the party of the ex-judge, Don Francisco Aguilar, the man my father is in prison for killing."

They rode on in silence for a while, each engrossed in his own thoughts. Ramon was deciding how to continue with his explanations, and draw from his companion the remaining details he required without arousing his hostility. Cánovas had been a schoolmaster in Málaga until his transformation to the first great statesman of the country. A historian and sometime journalist, Cánovas had been the author and inspiration behind the relative stability the country had experienced over the past few years. He was squint-eyed with a tic, and had an unprepossessing appearance wearing appalling clothes, hence his nickname 'the monster'. He was not a democrat by nature but realised that if Spain was to develop in peace, then it would have to be, in theory at least, a democracy. He was also a conservative but of the centre rather than on the far right. Together with the liberal leader, Práxedes Sagasta, who was also of the centre, he formed a pact in which each party would be allowed to rule in turn. This turn and turn about system had worked, was still working, because in reality there was little difference in the policies of the two men. This system, the *turno pacífico,* peaceful rota, was the one in which Ramon, as a member of the liberal party of Sagasta, was involved. The mayor of Sedella, who he had been sent to defend, was also a member of the liberal party.

"Cánovas may be of the right," Ramon began at last, "but he has brought stability. We can now choose our governments in peace without the army interfering, and we liberals are often in Government, as we are at present."

Whilst he knew this to be true, Ramon also knew that it left more unsaid than said. The *turno pacífico* satisfied neither the extreme right or left, or any of the many other factions present in the country. The Falangists, the Church, Carlists, Marxists, Anarchists, Republicans, Basque and Catalan Nationalists, and others left out of the 'pious fraud' were daily growing more and more restless.

The system was held in place by the local parties rigging the elections, to ensure that each party won in turn. In Sedella, as in all other small towns, this was controlled by two local *caciques*, bosses, one from each party, who made sure that the correct party won at the right time. The *cacique* of the party whose turn it was to rule nationally became mayor of the pueblo at the same time. The system of *caciquismo*, dominance of the local boss, brought about a strange condition in the rural pueblos, like Sedella, where it was most practised. This was a condition of political life where politics ran 'like an express train' through them, stopping only at election time when apathy took over, as the results were always known before the event. Ramon knew all this, even if Paco did not fully understand the extent of it. What he did not know, however, and could not know, was the tensions and conflicts caused by this system would lead eventually to the Civil War of 1936.

The two men reached the ford at Valverde where the river, which was usually just a shallow stream, was in full flood, and they had to force their horses through, the water coming up to the level of their stirrups. Once over the river, they rode up the final slope before the village. Directly ahead of them now, beyond the pueblo, was the mountain of Maroma, its summit obscured by a large white cloud. Paco explained that this cloud, which appeared to neither move or vary in size despite the fresh wind, was a common sight in the area and could remain there for days on end.

It was time, Ramon decided, to ask a crucial question, one he had been leading up to during all their time together. "Why was so much heat raised by a small piece of land?" he enquired. "Surely it was not worth much, and had been in dispute for many years, why the agitation?"

Paco glanced across at him. "It was an olive and almond grove, and there was a good undamaged house on it," he replied simply.

That short statement told the lawyer all he needed to know to understand why the small piece of land had had so much value and significance attached to it. He well knew the events of the past few years, and their consequences, that put a premium on such property.

Two years before, in 1884, Christmas had been celebrated as normal all over the local region, Sedella included. On Christmas Eve, the village folk had had their traditional meals and then attended midnight mass in the normal way. Christmas Day had dawned bright and sunny, and the village had been quiet as the inhabitants slept off their late night. Some goats went out as normal on that Thursday morning, a little late, to pasture on the hills above the village. Later still, a few farmers took their mules into the *campo* to work on their land. In the late afternoon, the whole village was astir and all the men and animals were returning.

At 8.56 p.m., sometime after nightfall, the village, together with all the surrounding area, was shaken by a *gran terremoto*, a severe earthquake. There was a loud rumbling and the ground shook, many buildings collapsed in part or whole, the church was severely damaged and most of its tower ruined. Incredibly, nobody was killed despite the amount of damage done. People ran out into the streets in panic, and there was much shouting and confusion. During the coming hours, days and even weeks, well into the New Year, lesser aftershocks were felt but little more structural damage was done.

During the following year, whilst the village struggled to rebuild the damaged buildings, two more disasters occurred.

The water supply, which had been disrupted by the earthquake, became contaminated by sewage and there was an outbreak of cholera. The onset was sudden and extreme, first one person, then another became ill with violent diarrhoea and vomiting. Within hours, deaths began to occur as the epidemic spread through the village.

The second disaster followed later that same year. There was an outbreak of *filoxera*, phylloxera, amongst the grape vines, in the whole of the Axarquía. The spread of this, which is caused by an aphid that feeds on the roots of the vine so killing the plant, was rapid and severe, bringing about the death of virtually all the vines in the area.

Before these three *trastornos*, Sedella had had a population of nearly 2000, a figure that had remained fairly stable for many years. The combined effects of these disasters however reduced the number by over half, by death and by migration to South America, to escape the poverty brought by the ruin of both homes and crops.

The knowledge of these events explained to Ramon the significance of the simple sentence of Paco. Land which was under the cultivation of almonds and olives and not grapes, and which had a house undamaged by the earthquake, was worth much at the present time. The families of the two local *caciques* were therefore both anxious to claim ownership. The reason for the heated quarrel over the decision of ex-judge Don Francisco Aguilar, whilst still in office, to transfer it back from one to the other was clear.

The two travellers arrived at the village in the afternoon, entering it close to the fountain where they dismounted and let their horses drink in the trough. The lawyer then went to talk to the deputy mayor who was standing in for the arrested man. From there, he was taken to the prison cell in the barracks of the Guardia Civil, where the accused men had been held since their arrest.

The lawyer was then able to listen to their story at first hand, and finalise his defence before returning a few days later to the coast at Torrox, under whose jurisdiction Sedella then was. Some days later, the accused men were also transferred to Torrox and the trial held.

The eventual discharge of all the accused except the mayor, who was only given a short sentence, owed more to the fact that they were of the same party as the national government, who appointed the judges, than to the efforts of Ramon in their defence. One is not a *cacique* for nothing, as Brennan remarks (in 'South from Granada') when describing a similar case of a mayor accused of murder in Yegen in the Alpujarras.

The case however altered the pueblo, the families of both *caciques* being forced to leave the village. The relatives of the murdered man left because of the backlash generated against them by the liberals, who remained in power until 1890. The mayor himself, on his release from prison, left the country and joined the exodus to South America.

Ramon, who retained an interest in the pueblo because of his involvement in the case, returned several times to visit Paco and various other friends he had made there. During these visits, he watched the gradual rebuilding of the village in both physical and human terms. Over the years, he witnessed the slow recovery take place, until by 1922 the pueblo was once more restored to some sort of normality. In that same year, the dictatorship of Primo de Rivera also brought about a period of stability in the country at large. The only building of note in the village not fully repaired was the church, which was to be further damaged in the Civil War, and finally demolished and rebuilt in the 1960's, long after Ramon's death.

The lawyer knew however that if the pueblo had recovered from the local *trastornos*, those of the nation had only been submerged and controlled by Primo. Ramon was not to live to see them once more erupt, this time with unparalleled violence and destruction, in the Civil War.

CHAPTER 12

EL PRONUNCIAMIENTO
(MILITARY UPRISING)

After the end of the Peninsular War when Bonaparte had been defeated, Spain returned to some sort of order. The liberal government that had led the opposition to the French occupying forces from Cádiz was overthrown, and the monarchy restored. A sort of stability and peace then ensued with, in the main, rule being shared between the two main parties under the monarch. A few army coups took place from time to time, with the country returning to stagnancy when the dust had died down. If things were fairly static politically, then so was the economy. Then, towards the end of the nineteenth century, this system began to come apart because of a growing number of stresses.

The Spanish empire in South America was disintegrating; regionalism in the country was growing; radicalism of many sorts was on the increase; labour disputes became endemic; assassinations of leading figures were a problem and the influence of unrest in Eastern Europe, especially from Russia, was threatening the status quo.

Then, in 1921, the troubles in the North African land governed by Spain brought a final disaster. At Annal in Morocco, the Berbers rose up and defeated the Spanish army, killing about ten thousand Spanish troops. The Spanish general, Silvestre, who had been personally selected by the King, against the advice of his ministers, committed suicide. The King was held to blame for the disaster, and to help stave off criticism, he set up an enquiry into the disaster. In September of 1923, however, before its publication, the army led by General Miguel Primo de Rivera rose up in a coup and issued a *Pronunciamiento*. There hadn't been one for many years, and it was to be the last before Mora delivered the one that led to the Civil War.

The King, Alfonso, who was dragged from his bed to be given the news, accepted the coup, and Primo set up a new administration after dissolving the *Cortes,* parliament.

Primo was a dictator but unlike many such was not a violent or vindictive man. During his reign, he did not have any of his political foes executed. He came from Andalucían aristocratic stock and was a popular man with most Spaniards, renowned for his personal generosity and courtesy. He was referred to as a benevolent dictator by nearly everyone. Despite this, censorship was strict and order restored throughout the country. He made a pact with the PSOE, the Spanish Socialist Party, and Francisco Largo Caballero, who was a socialist union president, became a minister in the government. Caballero was later to become a leading opponent of Franco during the Civil War.

Primo de Rivera was a moderniser and brought many improvements to Spain, especially to the infrastructure of the country. He undertook a vast building programme which included roads, ports and harbours, dams, electric power plants, and a network of distribution networks to deliver the power. He encouraged the selling of Spain as a tourist destination and opened a state-run chain of hotels, the *Paradores*, which are still in existence and thriving today. These *Paradores* were originally meant to be available for the use of the ordinary traveller, today however they are at the luxury end of the market. He opened the first of these at Gredos, near Madrid, in 1928. He was also not shy of taking on large foreign owned companies, and nationalised the oil industry, forming the state run firm of CAMPSA, the petroleum company. Education was also one of his ways of improving the lot of the ordinary Spaniard and providing qualified workers in the future. In the past, especially in the rural areas, the ruling classes had not seen the need for the labouring and peasant classes to read and write, let alone go on to any advanced level of learning. Schools, especially in the villages, were simply required to teach the Scriptures. Primo built many rural schools, and started to train teachers to fill them and make the lower classes literate. In this reform, he came into conflict with the big landowners who didn't want their labourers to become educated. He also clashed with the aristocracy, who owned most of the land of rural Spain, when he tried to bring in land reforms. It was the old divide in Spain reopening once again, modernisation versus the status quo.

In the end, this tension between the regime and the landowners, and Primo's lack of a grasp of economics that left many of his projects without funds, was to bring his dictatorship to an end. He had however released forces of progression and given the lower orders some vision, as well as improved living conditions. The tensions created by these advances, and the repressive forces of both the aristocracy and the Church, were in the end to lead to the Civil War.

In the pueblo, many of his reforms had little effect. The road to the village was not built until the 1960's; there was no power in the village, no state-run hotel built. What did affect it, however, was a change in the schooling of the children. A generation of literate and numerate men and women was the result. This change was reversed when Franco came to power, and the school reverted to simply the teaching of the Scriptures. When I first came to the village, many of the older men and women could read and write, having benefitted from Primo's reforms, whilst their children, the middle-aged and young adults, couldn't. Their children and those who had gone to school from the late 1970's onwards (post Franco) once again were literate. I know several adults who learned enough to be able to pass their driving test, where a certain level of literacy is required. Numeracy, however, was not such a problem as they could translate prices from pesetas to duros and back with rapid ease. A duro was a preferred local 'currency', which had a value of five pesetas. Try as I might, I could not translate say 17 duros into pesetas, or 215 pesetas into duros as quickly as the 'innumerate' locals, despite being a reasonably proficient mathematician.

The ancient car came to a spluttering halt in the square of the small town of Canillas de Aceituno, and its passenger got out. The driver also alighted, unstrapped two boxes from the roof, putting them down beside the young man, who was fumbling in his pocket to find money for the fare. The driver took the coins into his hand, spat on them and put them into his pocket, and then disappeared into the nearby bar.

The young man looked around the square, quiet in the early afternoon siesta, and then slowly followed the driver into the bar. His journey was almost over.

Óscar Mota y Gil was the newly appointed teacher to the school in Sedella, and on his way to take up his post. It had been a long and tiring journey. He had left Málaga early in the morning and travelled by the slow local train along the coast to Torre del Mar, where he had changed on to the line going inland, and taken the next train to the nearby town of Vélez-Málaga. Here, he had unloaded his two boxes and gone to look for a taxi. After a long search, he had found Ignacio, owner of an old Ford, and bartered a fare for the journey up the narrow windy road to Canillas. After driving along the bottom of a wide valley, the car had taken a lane on the right and driven up a steep, narrow winding road, with precipitous drops off first one side and then the other, before finally reaching the town.

In the bar, he ordered a brandy and asked about transport to take himself and his two boxes, at present still on the side of the road outside, to Sedella. After much animated discussion between all the customers in the bar, the barman sent his young son to find Adolfo, who Óscar was assured would be the best man to do the job. Peace and quiet returned to the bar and two brandies later Adolfo came in, wakened from his post lunch siesta by the boy. After listening to Óscar and examining the two boxes, he said there were two options. Either Óscar could walk beside Adolfo and his mule, which would carry the boxes, or a second mule could be used for Óscar himself to ride.

"How far away is Sedella?" Óscar enquired.

"About eight or so kilometres," Adolfo answered. "It's an easy walk."

At this point, several customers at the bar offered differing views. "There's a big hill to climb," said one. "It is an easy walk though," agreed another. "Not in this heat," yet another. The noise level and arguments rose.

In the end, it was decided that Óscar would hire two mules, one to ride and one to carry his boxes.

Adolfo left the bar to get his beasts, and the taxi driver, after pouring water into his radiator which had overheated on the climb up to the village, drove off down the hill, leaving Óscar standing in the warm September afternoon sunshine waiting for Adolfo. At last they set off, with the two boxes strapped to the *angarillas* on one mule, and Óscar astride the second, with Adolfo hanging on to its tail.

They dropped down from the town to just above the *Río Almanchares*, which the mule track then followed along the side of the valley. Opposite a small mill almost at the end of the valley, the track went down to the stream, crossed it and zigzagged up the high steep side of the valley. At the top a *puerto,* pass, took them out onto the side of another valley. The track then wound its way along the contour, over a rise and past the junction with the track to Valverdes, a small hamlet some way away, and then finally reached Sedella.

It was nearly dark when Óscar finally managed to find the small house that had been rented for him by the school authorities. Tired and hungry, he found his way to the *plaza* in front of the church and into a bar, where he was able to order a meal. Whilst he was eating it, he was found by the *alcalde,* Diego Aguila y Martín, who had been warned of his arrival by the *Junta de Málaga*. With Diego was a young woman, Lidia, also an outsider, who had arrived a few days earlier and was to be his assistant teacher. The next day, the mayor took him to see the school, a low stone building opposite a mill in a small *calle,* street, at the edge of the pueblo. Previous to his appointment, the school had only opened three days a week for children between five and ten, and had been run by the priest. Now, under the new arrangements brought in by Primo de Rivera, it would be open for five days every week, and take children up to fourteen years of age. The priest would attend for one day each week to teach the Scriptures. Diego warned the two new teachers that they might face some hostility from the priest, because of his reduced role in the school, and from some of the local farmers who wanted to use their children on the land as they had always done in the past.

"Especially those over ten," the mayor said. "That's when their schooling used to stop, and there is much work to be done in the *campo*. The people are poor and cannot afford to pay labourers. I will help all I can, as education is important and necessary for the future."

Two days later, the school opened and the children came cautiously into the room, wary of the two outsiders. Soon, however, most of them were excitedly joining in the lesson. When they realised they would not be made to repeat the catechism and religious texts as they had done under the stern eye of Don Fernando, the priest, but that they were to learn the alphabet and write it on their own slates in chalk, the teachers got their attention.

During the first few weeks, because of the novelty value, there were few problems. The children enjoyed scratching letters on to their slates, learning to read their first few words from the books they had been given, and looking at the maps of Spain, Europe and the world that they were shown. After this, it was harder work to keep their attention. Problems arose between the quick learners and their slower peers, and between those who enjoyed learning and those who saw no point in it. Things were not helped by the removal of children to help on the land or in the home, or by the attitude of the priest, Don Fernando.

When the first term came to an end at Christmas, both Óscar and Lidia were more than relieved. Then loneliness set in. They were going to stay in the pueblo for the short break, and both spent a fairly miserable Christmas Eve alone, whilst all around them the villagers enjoyed their family meals. They went to mass at midnight, and for the first time met some of the locals. They had been too busy preparing lessons and organising the new school to have had much time or energy left for socialising. The villagers were not used to lone outsiders living in their midst, and had made little or no effort on their part to get to know them.

On Christmas day itself, the village was quiet and empty as many people were out working in the *campo* whilst others slept off the results of over indulgence. Lidia spent much of the day indoors, reading and regretting her isolation, whilst Óscar went for a solitary walk in the sierra. As they had not mixed with the locals during their busy first term, their isolation was only to be expected.

They had also not made much effort to get to know each other. Óscar was a bit of a loner in any case, a 26 year old man from Málaga who had at one time been in a seminary studying for the priesthood, before changing course to qualify as a teacher. Lidia had been born and brought up in Granada, and was a shy 19 year old. She was too young and self-conscious to try to mix with strangers. It was only in front of a class that she lost her inhibitions.

The breakthrough came on the following day, the 26th.

Nerieda was a precocious child, and had been a thorn in the side of both her teachers all that first term. At fourteen, she was a well-developed young woman, both physically and mentally. She had left school at ten, and now at fourteen was being forced back for a year. If the *alcalde*, Diego, hadn't been a member of the socialist party and an avid supporter of education, then she may have been able to avoid being re-schooled. But his decree was for all children of the relevant age range to go to school, and his writ was law in the pueblo, and was enforced by the town councillors to a man. Precocious, rebellious and obstinate, she had made the two teachers' lives uncomfortable, to say the least, during their first term. She also fancied Óscar, even though he was much older than her and she was in his eyes still a child, and one that was in his care. This obvious treatment of her as child and not woman made her even more troublesome to him, despite or perhaps because of the attraction she felt for him.

On the 26th, she met him in the street, where he was mooching along dispiritedly in very low spirits. She was dressed up and had been with her younger brother Ivan to see their aunt, who lived a few streets away, and he didn't recognise her. Óscar did however know Ivan and they got into a conversation. Nerieda found Óscar was, out of school, funny and interesting to talk to, whilst he, thinking she was some older relative of Ivan's, in his turn found her charming and gracious. She knew he hadn't recognised her and invited him back to their home for tea. He was taken aback, confused and totally embarrassed when she introduced him to her parents as their teacher. Fortunately, they all saw the funny side of the situation, and the ice was broken.

This chance encounter and Óscar's subsequent introduction to Ivan and Nerieda's family was to be the beginning of the two teachers' acceptance by the people of the pueblo. On New Year's Eve, they both went to a party at Nerieda's parents' home.

School became easier to teach and control after the Christmas break. Nerieda became less of a problem, in fact she began to take her studies seriously and went on to Málaga when she was fifteen to continue studying. This, together with the acceptance by the locals and the support of the mayor, made the two teachers' task less troublesome. A whole generation would benefit from the efforts of Lidia, Óscar and the teachers who followed them, up until the time that the school, along with many others, was once more reduced to simply teaching the catechism.

When Nerieda grew up, she too was to become a teacher and meet up again with Óscar in Madrid, when they were both fighting against the Nationalist army. Together they escaped to Mexico, along with many others when the capital fell into the rebels' hands.

Óscar's wife, who he had married some years after leaving the village, was killed in the war as was Lidia. Despite the age difference, Óscar and Nerieda married whilst living in Mexico, and returned to Sedella for a visit to her family and their friends after the death of Franco. On this journey to the pueblo, Óscar didn't have to ride on a mule but came all the way from Málaga by bus, on the road which was extended to the village in the 1960's.

CHAPTER 13

EL EXTRANJERO
(The foreigner)

El extranjero, an Englishman, had sailed from Dover to La Coruña, in Galicia, on the steamship Hollandia, landing in Spain on 28th September 1919. Recently demobilised from the army, after a distinguished period serving in the Great War, during which he was awarded both the MC and the Croix de Guerre for his time in the Cyclists' Battalion, his plan was to travel to southern Spain, rent a house in either the Axarquía or the Alpujarras, and take up writing full time. From La Coruña he travelled slowly on foot and by train to Madrid, where he stayed two days, and then left for Granada which he reached on 10th October.

Spain in those days had poor roads, mainly all unsurfaced, but a large network of *ferrocarriles,* railways. The problem with these 'iron-roads' was that the trains on them, even the expresses, only travelled at between 8 to 10 miles per hour. This was little better than going by bike in his opinion, based on his war time experiences.

In the end, when he finally reached Granada it was raining and the city was a vast disappointment to him. He thought that the Alhambra was splendid but shoddy, and appeared to him to be bedraggled. It was like an exotic gypsy girl sheltering behind a damp and dismal hedge. The people too were a disappointment to his romanticised ideas. They were not, as he had envisaged and expected, men wearing long cloaks with daggers protruding from their belts, and statuesque women wearing *mantillas* and with hair held by combs. They were glum and with short legs, and rushed past him sheltering under umbrellas. They talked in raucous loud voices until the early morning, and never seemed to sleep.

His stay in Granada was therefore short and wet, and the following day after lunch he set out to walk to the coast. At first the rain held off, and taking the rough track south-westwards out of the city, he soon passed through Armilla. By the time he reached Gabia la Grande, about fifteen kilometres from Granada, the rain was falling heavily again. The road ran straight ahead through the barren *vega*, at times knee deep in mud, made worse by the constant passage of wagons drawn by teams of mules.

When he reached La Malahá, the evening was already drawing in and he was soaked to the skin. The last nine kilometres to Ventas de Huelma were made in the dark, during which time the rain stopped, the sky cleared and the stars came out.

After leaving Ventas de Huelma, he set out on the final part of his journey to visit the Axarquía in the first stage of his search for a place to live. The village of Sedella was his first port of call.

◊ ◊ ◊ ◊ ◊

El extranjero reached the crest of the Sierra Tejeda in the late afternoon. The sun which had been shining all day from a clear, almost brilliant blue sky was already low on the western horizon to his right. All morning he had walked, from the small rural *parador* in Ventas de Huelma to the base of the sierra, a distance of some twenty-five kilometres, toiling through a barren landscape still scarred from the earthquake of 1884, nearly forty years earlier. Despite being October the sun was hot, the way arduous, and he was soon bathed in sweat. He passed through the villages of Agrón and Arenas del Rey, both places he thought to be dreary, run down and shoddily built settlements. The people in these villages were wary of strangers and unfriendly. In both of them he tried to buy some refreshments, bread and some cheese or ham to eat, perhaps coffee to drink, but there did not seem to be any shops, bars, or cafes. In the end, he had to settle for water obtained from the village fountains, near which women were gathered collecting water and washing clothes in the adjacent sinks. As he approached to fill his bottle at the continually running pipe, they fell silent and glanced sideways at him in curiosity. As he left the village behind, he could hear their chatter recommence.

For a long period after passing through the last of the villages he met no-one at all, except a half-witted youth tending a herd of black Spanish pigs, whose gibbering language was unintelligible. All

118

afternoon, he had climbed up the steep-sided mountain through a jumble of rocks. He scrambled over screes of loose stones, to the summit over two thousand and eight hundred feet above the *vega* he had just left. Throughout the afternoon, during this climb, he saw no other human being at all but spied much wildlife. All around there were rabbits and some hares, and in the distance he saw several ibex and deer, and once he came upon a small group of wild boar which scattered, startled, from his path. He had hardly got over the shock that this event gave him when he almost trod on a large black snake, asleep on the path ahead. Once woken, the snake slid away, harmless but unnerving in its silent retreat. Overhead, he saw the occasional Griffon vulture, a few buzzards and a pair of golden eagles, but no small birds amongst the arid stones.

Below and behind him as he climbed he could see a scattering of distant *cortijos,* farmsteads, each surrounded by plantations of olive trees and fertile strips of land. Tall poplar trees followed the line of the watercourses in the deep, steep-sided valleys which ran down the hillside and over the distant plain. The ground over which he toiled however was dry and rocky, the only vegetation growing on it being the wild evergreen dwarf ilexes or holm oak native to the area. Near the top even these could not exist, leaving only bare rock whose glistening mica bands quickly lost their sparkle as the sun dropped below the crest of the hill.

The map he carried was totally inadequate and only marked villages, roads, streams and rivers, but not the mountains or the mule tracks or *senderos,* footpaths, like the one he was following. As there were hardly any roads in the area, only mule tracks, the villages were shown as unconnected isolated dots. Because of this, he lost his way many times during the course of the day. However, when he reached the top of the climb, he found himself almost exactly at the point that he had intended.

The low weakening sun now gave very little heat and this, together with the evening breeze, quickly cooled off his sweat and chilled his aching body. As he stood shivering on the crest some six thousand eight hundred feet above sea level, he could see the whole of the Axarquía spread out below, and beyond it the Mediterranean sea, and hazy on the far horizon the coastline of Africa, with the low mountains a dull purple in the slowly dying sunlight.

Immediately below could be seen the nearest villages of the district, splashes of white dotted about on the pale red foothills, and in the far distance the larger towns of Vélez- Málaga and Torre del Mar at the end of the rocky fingers of the lower slopes, as they fell in a succession of ridges, waves and cones to the shoreline. Over each village columns of smoke were rising and fanning out, and as his body chilled off, he fancied he could even smell the sweet acrid wood smoke and feel its warmth.

By reference to the map, despite its inadequacy, he was able to pick out Sedella, his destination, as being the nearest of the visible villages. Between himself and this village he could see herds of goats and sheep with their shepherds, slowly making their way back either to the pueblo or to the rough huts used by them on the hillside. The sounds of the goat bells carried easily to him on the quiet mountain air. Without a thought for the coming darkness or a further pause for reflection, he plunged quickly down the steep slope towards the village.

He had travelled from Granada to Ventas de Huelma, where he had spent a night before starting for Sedella that morning. The *parador* at Huelma, a stopping place for the muleteers, was built in traditional Andalucían style, with large double entrance doors leading into a cobbled yard with a vaulted ceiling. Around this were stables, a kitchen and living areas. He had joined the *arrieros,* the muleteers, who were already at the *parador* waiting for their evening meal. This when it came was *arroz y bacalao,* rice and salt cod, served in a large brown stoneware dish, which was placed centrally on the table. Each person then produced their own spoon and ate from the section in front of him, leaving a thin wall of food between his portion and that of his neighbour.

It had been a strange and solemn meal to the Englishman, each *arriero* keeping his hat firmly on his head during its course and, at its conclusion, washing his own spoon and replacing it in his *faja,* a red flannel waistband. This ritual of the meal, which was carried out in silence and with both gravity and courtesy between the muleteers, had pleased *el extranjero*, who considered that at last he had arrived in the real Spain, that of a Spanish grandee who asserted his equality to everyone at the table and ate with great courtesy and formality.

The next morning, after a good night's sleep, assisted by the soporific sounds of the mules and donkeys in the adjacent stables stamping and whickering, and with the sun shining overhead, he had set out with a light heart towards the south. In the distance, he could see the Sierra Tejeda, which he must cross, some thirty kilometres away.

Before leaving the *parador* its proprietor, a short, fat grey-haired Andalucían, advised him to cross the mountains just to the east of the summit of Maroma, and then drop down into the pueblo of Sedella where, he declared, there was a good *posada*. This *posada,* he stated, was used by the *arrieros* who brought strings of mules carrying salt and salt cod over the mountain range from the coast to Granada, returning by the same route carrying goods from Granada to sell in the villages of the Axarquía.

The Englishman had made a strange figure as he strode out through the early sunlight being thin, over six feet tall, and dressed in flannel trousers, tweed coat and a firm-brimmed black hat of the Córdoba style, and carrying a small rucksack. He had bought the wide brimmed hat in Granada to make himself less conspicuous!

Night fell as he scrambled down the steep sides of the sierra towards Sedella, but fortunately not until he had descended the first steep slopes, some of which were almost vertical rock faces, perhaps some twenty feet long at each drop, and needed careful negotiation. Below these drops were sharp-sided ridges covered with cruel spined bushes and loose scree slopes. Lower still, when it was full dark, the route was fortunately easier, passing through groves of ilexes and pines. Nearer the village there were walnut, carob and mulberry trees. His route took him past the tiny square stone hut at the lower end of a steep pipeline in which a small wheel, turned by the force of the water rushing down the pipe, generated six volt electricity for the pueblo below. He was seen by several lone shepherds as he stumbled towards the village, but never thought to stop and seek them out and ask to stay the night, as a more prudent course than trying to reach

121

the village. One who saw him was Esteban Ruíz, a local goatherd, who was in his corral but too busy to call out and invite the stranger in to shelter for the night, as he was engaged in helping one of his goats deliver twin kids.

The Englishman however noticed none of the locals that he passed, or the small 'power station' in his headlong dash down to Sedella in the dark. He also passed close to the mill situated just above the village, but this too he also failed to notice.

It was very late, gone 10 pm, when he at last reached Sedella, soaked in sweat, scratched and bleeding from many small cuts, and with his clothes torn. He entered the pueblo by a footpath that took him close to the village fountain and washing place, deserted at that time of night. Heading through the village, he came at last to the small square in front of the church where there was a bar. Here he ordered a glass of brandy, and asked directions to the *parador* that had been recommended by the innkeeper in Ventas de Huelma. He struggled to make sense of the reply, whilst he was examined with curiosity by the other customers in the bar. No *extranjero* had been seen in the pueblo in living memory, though many villagers themselves had been to France or Switzerland seeking work. The strange tall Englishman, dirty, weary and covered in small cuts, and wearing a formal Córdoba type hat, was an odd sight indeed. Although he had had little trouble understanding the language in Madrid, or even in Granada, the rural Andalucían of the pueblo was proving to be almost impenetrable to him, and he stood puzzling over the barman's reply. He was a scholar of both Greek and Latin and could speak French, he had indeed been a translator during part of the war, he could also speak some German and Italian, and so whilst Castilian Spanish had presented few problems, here in the small village bar it was another matter.

At last, he managed to decipher the meaning of the reply that the barman, together with now most of his customers, was trying to get across to him. The 'good *posada*' no longer existed; there was only the smaller poorer one in the village, belonging to María Dolores del Río in the *Calle de Andalucía*. Finishing his brandy, he followed the directions they gave him and went back the way he had come down the badly cobbled street, and turned right into the *Calle de Andalucía*.

The streets were lit by the dim glow of the bulbs whose power was derived from the small generator he had passed, unnoticed, on the hillside above the village.

He hammered on the door of the *posada*, waking the old widow María. She awoke grumbling from her sleep to let him in, and made him a simple meal of two eggs, fried in rancid oil, bread of surprisingly good quality, and reheated coffee. As he settled down to an exhausted sleep, disturbed by the army of bugs in the bed, he thought that here, in the heart of rural Axarquía, he was at last getting to grips with the country.

In the morning, after a breakfast of bread and coffee, he made enquiries as to where he could get his clothes repaired after the ravages of the day before. María Dolores directed him to the house of her niece who agreed to repair and wash his shirt, trousers and coat for a small sum, and have them ready for the next day. Wearing the spare clothes from his rucksack, he then explored the village and surrounding area.

He found that the pueblo itself was similar to most in the Axarquía, consisting of stone-built houses rendered and painted white, with either shallow pitched red tile roofs or flat terraced ones. They were generally of two or three storeys. Most were built on slopes with the lower floor, the basement, opening out at ground level on the lower side, whilst the first floor opened at ground level further up the slope. The lower floor was usually an *almacen*, store, and also usually a stable, whilst the upper floors were the living areas. In the basement area crops were kept, barrels of local wine stored and chickens and mules housed. The streets were narrow, cobbled with many steps in them, and littered with goat, sheep and mule droppings.

Immediately surrounding the town were many small fertile plots, or *bancales*, on which were grown maize, wheat, barley and a variety of vegetables. These plots were irrigated by a network of small water courses, almost certainly dating back in their conception to Moorish or even Roman times. Further away from the village, the sides of the steep valleys were cultivated with vines, whose fruit was used to produce both raisins and the sweet Málaga wine referred to in the village as *terreno*. There were olive and almond groves, occasional fig,

123

walnut and mulberry trees, along with some carob trees whose chocolate-like fruit was used as animal fodder. Just outside the village, he also came across a Roman hump-backed bridge at the start of a mule track leading over the sierras to Alhama de Granada which, if he had known of its existence, would have made his journey of the day before much easier and quicker, Alhama and Ventas de Huelma being about twenty-six kilometres apart on the other side of the hill.

The posada provided a good lunch of local *serrano* ham, goat's cheese and fruit, and a more substantial evening meal than the one of the previous night, of soup, goat's meat and once again fruit. The cost of the two nights stay came to just a few pesetas.

The following morning, he collected his newly washed and repaired clothes from María's niece and, having decided that the Axarquía was not where he wished to live, being too rugged, he left the pueblo. He wanted to live in an area which was better irrigated and more diversified. He therefore descended via Valverde and Vélez-Málaga to the coast at Torre del Mar, and turned eastwards towards Motril, to go and explore the Alpujarras where he was finally to settle in the village of Yegen.

No record of his stay in Sedella survived, except for a few local memories and a short mention in his book 'South from Granada'.

El extranjero was of course Gerald Brennan.

CHAPTER 14

LA GUERRA CIVIL
(The Civil War)

In 1936, two Spanish generals Goded and Mola, under the nominal leadership of the exiled general Sanjurjo, led the uprising and the revolt of the army that was to start the *Guerra Civil*. Franco, who was to eventually become the leader, did not join the revolt until sometime later. In fact, Mola was said to be so irritated by Franco's dithering that he said 'with or without *Francito* (little Franco, a name hated by Franco), we will go ahead'. This reluctance on his part to join the revolt at its inception, but instead to wait and see if it was successful or not, did not stop Franco from having another general shot for the same reason.

The uprising by the army was supposed to take place on the 18th of July at 5 am in Morocco, in response to a telegram from Mola which read 'on the 15th last at 5 am, Helena gave birth to a beautiful child'. However like much in Spain, indeed in the general confusion that surrounds any such event, things did not go entirely to plan and the army garrison in Melilla rose up a day early. Franco then belatedly joined the rebels, and later would become the sole leader, after both Mola and Goded were killed in separate aeroplane crashes.

The Civil War was to be fought between the many factions and along the fault lines that had developed in Spanish society over the previous centuries. On the one side was the army, the large landowners, much of the Church, the Carlists, the Falange and other right wing groups. Ranged against them were the Liberal Republicans, the Socialists, Communists, anarchists and the separatist movements of both Catalan and the Basque. The Church in the Basque region was mainly on the side of the Republic, unlike in the rest of Spain.

Some of these divisions were also a cause of strife and tension within both sides of the struggle. Franco, for instance, disposed of the leaders of the Carlists and the Falange, finally merging all the various factions on the Nationalist side into one *Movimiento,* Movement, with

125

himself at its head. The Republican parties also sometimes squabbled amongst themselves, as did the communists and anarchists, actually fighting each other during the course of the war.

The war was also supported by outside countries, with Hitler's Germany and Mussolini's Italy joining the Nationalists, and Russia the Republicans. The western nations remained neutral, a position many claim made the Second World War more inevitable. These nations did however send many mercenaries who formed the 'International Brigades', which fought for the Republic against Franco.

In Sedella, most of the inhabitants were on the side of the Republic, and suffered for it by a cruel repression that lasted long after the conflict had ceased, right up until just before Franco's death on Thursday November 20th in 1975. During this period of repression in the village, some inhabitants spent most of it living as outlaws on the slopes of the sierras. One such used to take his small flock of goats along the track past our house during our first few years here. He was an educated man, said to be a poet before the war, and would go into a bar for a coffee after his evening meal and read the daily paper. Many families were split apart by the conflict and some still bear the scars to this day. The following story is a tribute to the villagers who defied the venom of Franco.

◊　◊　◊　◊　◊

The small band of *Guardia Civil,* civil guard (a rural police force), toiled in single file up the narrow path out of the pueblo. Already the early morning July sun was hot, and the guards in their coarse green uniforms were perspiring heavily. The five men and their sergeant were all from the north of Spain and this, together with their heavy uniforms, rigid black tri cornered bat-winged hats worn in all weathers, and the heavy Mauser rifles and knapsacks they all carried, made them unsuited for the hot southern sun and steep mountain slopes.

The Guardia were formed in 1844 by the government of Narváez out of the *Migueletes*, an early rural police force, to bring law and order to the bandit-ridden countryside of that time and to protect private property, especially that of the large landowners. The rule was that they were not allowed to serve in their own province, and in practice were usually sent to parts of the country to which their own area had an antipathy. In the recent *Guerra Civil,* Civil War, the Guardia had in the main fought on the side of Franco's Nationalist Army.

As the Guardia patrol left the village behind and laboured past the *bancales,* allotments, the locals working in them glanced sideways to watch them pass with silent resentment. Passing the mill above the village, they continued upwards into the tree-covered slope of the sierra.

High on the hillside above the village, the poet Salvador and his companions saw them coming. Before entering the trees, the file of the six Guardia had been clearly visible, the sun reflecting off their rifle barrels an added pointer to their progress.

Like many in Spain at this time, Salvador and his small group who lived on the mountain were in hiding, being supporters of and fighters for the Republican forces defeated in the war that had, a few years earlier, torn the country apart. Many had been killed in the war, both during and after it, and many more executed. Others had fled to France, Russia, Britain and South America, or to any other country that would accept them. All over Spain, like those on the hillside, even more were in hiding, unable to return to their homes for fear of arrest, and imprisonment or execution. Ronald Fraser in his book 'In Hiding' tells of Manuel Cortés, the ex-mayor of Mijas, a village not far from the mountain on which Salvador was sitting. He lived for almost thirty years in his own house, for long periods in a cupboard, without the knowledge of the rest of the people of Mijas.

The men on the mountainside watched the Guardia patrol disappear into the trees below with dispassionate amusement. The mountain with all its ridges, folds and paths were well known to them, and they could easily anticipate the route being followed by the guards. They also enjoyed the active support and help of the majority of the villagers, who fed them both information and sustenance on a day to day basis. From time to time, they caught a glimpse of the patrol or a flash of light from their weaponry, as they moved westwards along the hillside through the trees towards the *Río Almanchares*, above the gorge of *La Rahije* through which it flows.

Sitting on their rock in the sun, the small group of renegades had no fear of the Guardia foot patrols that from time to time were sent out from the village to hunt them down. Their local knowledge was extensive, and the expanse of the sierras open to them so vast that even the large scale hunts at the end of the *Guerra Civil* had had no chance of finding them. Over the years they had built a succession of small huts on the hillside and moved from one to another, so that no permanent signs of habitation were observable to their pursuers.

In the early days, the group had been kept alive by a constant supply of food sent up daily from the village by their friends and relations below, via the goatherds who grazed their flocks on the hills around them. The years after the war, however, were hard for the Spanish people, and food was short even in the small mainly self-sufficient villages of the countryside. These were known as the 'hungry years', made worse by Franco's deliberate policy of revenge and retribution in those areas which had been most hostile to his forces, like eastern Andalucía. In the country as a whole, rebuilding and development after the war was slow and food scarce. Foreign governments, especially those of Europe now embroiled in their own war, were mainly hostile to the new Spanish regime, and reluctant to give aid to or trade with it. Over time, however, the renegades had become more self-sufficient by hunting the prolific game in the area, and even keeping their own small flock of goats.

In this way, they had been able to help the inhabitants of the pueblo by supplying them with some of the meat from the game they hunted. This was especially useful as hunting was strictly controlled by the authorities, and firearm ownership forbidden to most people.

The group were also able to help the pueblo in another way. Shortly after the end of the war, the government autarchy had made esparto grass, a wild plant that grows over all the hillsides of the local sierras, into an official crop. The government restricted the rights to its picking to a few private businessmen in the province, and its plaiting was only allowed under license. Esparto grass is used extensively in the locality in the fabrication of ropes, shoes, mule harness and panniers, and in the production of both olive oil and wine. The grass is plaited into circular mats used in squeezing olives, and into long strips used when pressing grapes. Whilst it was therefore difficult, and even dangerous, for the villagers to leave the pueblo and cut and harvest esparto grass, the outlaws could do so with impunity. This they did, sending it down under cover of darkness, unknown to the Guardia who policed its use, in repayment for the support they were receiving from the villagers.

The Guardia sergeant leading the patrol was from Aragon province in the north, and like almost all of the Guardia he had fought in the Civil War for the Nationalist forces of Franco. He came from a poor family who lived in the countryside near Huesca and was a royalist by inclination. As such, he was a member of the Carlist party, *Comunión Tradicionalista* (CT). The CT supported Franco and joined his coalition against the Republican government. When, during the first year of the war, in December 1936, Franco disbanded the CT and amalgamated it into the Falange, effectively at the same time exiling its leader Manuel Fal Conde to Portugal and impugning the Royalist cause, the sergeant lost much of his ardour for the Nationalist cause. At the end of the war, when it had become increasingly clear that Franco had no intention of restoring the monarchy but intended to rule himself as a dictator, the sergeant's support for him was low indeed. He now felt more sympathy for the local peasantry who were, despite their obvious anarchist and communist leanings, very like those of his own family and region. He pursued his vain task of hunting out the local dissidents in the hills, therefore, with less than enthusiasm.

The sergeant had however under his command two young Catalans, members of the extreme right wing fascist party, *Juntas de Ofensiva Nacional Sindicalista* (JONS). They were, for all their youth, veterans of the vicious infighting of Barcelona that occurred before the uprising, and so he had to at least give a pretence of being eager to seek out the fugitives. He knew that these were dangerous days, and any outward show of sympathy to the local Republicans could lead to his own denunciation and arrest. He therefore drove his small patrol hard during the morning, before allowing them a rest at midday. Thankfully, when he called a halt the men, even the two JONS zealots, sank down in relief to rest and to allow the sun to dry out their damp sweaty clothes.

During the rest break, the sergeant discussed tactics with his corporal, an elderly Basque who had joined the Guardia long before the Civil War began. As a Basque Catholic, his sympathies throughout the war had been largely with the Republicans, however being already a member of a Guardia unit he had, for his own self preservation, fought for the Nationalist forces. Whilst the majority of the Catholic Church was in support of Franco and his fellow officers, in the Basque country they backed the Republican side that were, in their turn, sympathetic to the Basque's claim to independence. His position was like countless others in Spain during the war, who had to join the forces in control of their particular part of the country, regardless of their own feelings and sympathies. To do otherwise meant either to try to escape and join the opposite side, or risk imprisonment or death. The corporal's aim was now simply to serve out his time in the Guardia, and then return to his home town of Pamplona on his retirement.

After the rest, the sergeant planned to split his force into two, one led by himself and the other by the corporal, and head back in a westerly direction, slightly apart, to try and surprise the dissidents. Neither of them had any expectation of finding the rebels by this move, or any wish to either, but it kept the men busy and maintained a pretence that they were doing all they could.

During the morning, whilst the patrol was moving eastwards, Salvador and his companions had met up with two goatherds and exchanged both goods and news. The small group had lived on the hillside for a few years already, since the fall of Málaga to the Nationalist forces in the spring of 1937.

In January of that year the Nationalist forces, mainly composed of Italian 'volunteers' under the overall command of General Gonzalo Queipo de Llano y Sierra, the Spanish governor of Nationalist Andalucía, marched on Málaga. By the 17th of January they had reached Marbella to its west with little opposition. On the 5th of February, the continued advance from the west brought an evacuation of Málaga city and a flight eastwards along the coast by its Republican defenders.

At the same time the Italian Black Shirts, some ten thousand mechanised troops under General Roatta, reached the pass of Ventas de Zafarraya overlooking the coast road from Málaga to Almeria, along which the retreating forces and refugees were streaming. From these commanding heights, the Italian artillery conducted a bombardment of the fleeing Republicans.

Antonio, one of Salvador's comrades on the mountain above the pueblo, had been a member of the forces defending Málaga. During the course of the disastrous retreat from the city, he had left the main body of troops and returned to his home in the pueblo. He arrived in the village just prior to the first of the Italian troops, who had fanned out over the Axarquía to subdue the populace.

Salvador, the poet, was also in the pueblo at that time, in the role of an administrator for the republic. As a very young man, and a committed Republican, he had been politically active both before and during the war. In 1931, when the Second Republic was declared, he had been part of a group of youngsters who had joined older inhabitants and, fired by reforming zeal, had destroyed part of the village church already damaged by the earthquake of half a century earlier. Along with many others in Andalucía, they had taken part in the wave of anti-clericism that had swept the province. Their anger was more against the church authorities and the priests than against religion itself, and much of the damage was carried out in awe and fear of divine retribution. Many stories abound of communities destroying religious buildings and statues, and chasing out the priests, and then, later, carrying these same defaced and damaged statues round the streets in procession on various saint's days. They acted, as one foreigner observed, like naughty school children intent on mischief, defying a stern adult, yet looking over their shoulders to make sure they were not observed. Yet much damage was done, and many priests and nuns chased from the area and even killed. There was a false rumour circulated in Nationalist areas that naked nuns were crushed on the streets of Málaga by steamrollers.

At the start of the war, in 1936, Salvador was a prominent member of the *Union General de Trabajadores* (UGT), the socialist trades union that joined the popular front at that time. As one of the leading local members of the UGT, he was given the task of helping organise the village, and ensure the continuation of its life after the local right wing officials had either fled or been shot.

After the fall of Málaga these two, Salvador and Antonio, fled the village before the arrival of the Italian troops. They were joined in their exile on the sierra by one or two other fugitives who returned to the village at the end of hostilities. With the Italian troops came the return of the priest and other local dignitaries, together with some Nationalist troops. Those prominent local Republicans who had not, like Salvador and Antonio, fled the village were soon paying the price of their former alliance with the left wing cause. Some were hanged from the *'Torre del Omenaje'*, the Moorish tower in the village square. Some were shot against the cemetery wall to the east of the pueblo. It was against this wall that at least one woman died and a village youth, Manolo, had both his knees shot.

In the pueblo, as in most of the towns and villages throughout the length and breadth of Spain, the *Guerra Civil* split communities and families alike, bringing schisms that, in some cases, are still to be found today. Brother fought against brother, fathers and sons were turned against each other. Despite these splits the pueblo, like much of the region, was in the main in support of the republic. Many were communists and anarchists, whilst others were more moderate socialists or liberals. Some of the village were anti-Catholic and even perhaps fervent atheists, whilst others, though opposed to the priests, remained Catholics. Whatever the shade of opinion, the greater majority of the pueblo however supported the Second Republic, and were against the right wing Nationalist uprising. It was not long therefore before Salvador and his companions were in regular communication with the friends and relations they had left behind when they fled to the countryside. A state of affairs that was to continue to the time of the general amnesty of March 1969.

News of the movements of the two groups of the Guardia was brought to the hunted group by the son of one of the goatherds, who had seen the splitting of the patrol and subsequent change of direction take place shortly before. On hearing of the approach of the patrol from the boy, they withdrew further up the slope by way of the *Arroyo de la Fuente,* river of the fountain, which supplied water to the village below. From their new perch below the summit of Cuascuadra to the east of the towering peak of Maroma, they spent the afternoon trying to plot the route of the two groups of Guardia below them. Further below still, they could see the pueblo, a harsh white jumble of small houses dominated by the ruins of the old Moorish fort.

From time to time, during moonless nights, they visited the village singly to reunite for a short while with their nearby but remote families. On the walls of the village houses, they saw posters describing them as bandits and brigands, and offering rewards for their capture. Whilst there was indeed, in the Sierras de Ronda for instance, armed groups of bandits, mainly refugees from the war like themselves, here in the Sierra Tejeda things were different. Whilst in their youth they may have been political firebrands and, in the war, fighters for their cause, now they were a danger to no one. They were simply survivors of the war hunted for their past actions by a cold, cruel dictator. It was this fact of their non-aggression over the long years of exile that would allow them to return to the village after the amnesty, to take up their lives again after over 30 years of living in exile on the mountainside. In the same way Manuel Cortés, ex-mayor of Mijas some few miles away, would be able to emerge from his cupboard, to the astonishment of his neighbours, and rejoin the life of that town. All over the land in fact, the refugees would return and the whole country, a few years later, return to a normal democratic life. The man who was mayor of the pueblo when I first came to the village would himself be able to return from France, where had had to live since he joined the *Partido Socialista Obrero Español* (PSOE), the socialist party, in the 1960's when it was still an illegal organisation. Salvador, the poet, and his companions would come down from the mountain at last, Salvador himself to take up the life of a village goatherd.

Now, as the sun began to dip behind the ridge of hills to the west, the Guardia patrol linked up once again and made their way wearily back to the pueblo down the side of the *Loma de Cuascuadra* to the east of the village. The sergeant and corporal at least were pleased that they had had no sightings of their quarry. In a few weeks' time, they would once again make another fruitless search of the mountains, and so on with growing reluctance over the coming months and years. On entering the pueblo, they were ignored by the majority of villagers they met, who hurried past them with averted eyes. From behind semi-closed shutters, their route was observed with a mixture of resentment at their presence and humour at their tired, dishevelled state. The two Catalan privates seethed at their lack of success, and returned hostility with hostility in the glances they exchanged with those of the inhabitants who dared to look their way.

High on the hillside above, Salvador and his fellow fugitives made their way back to their latest living place to prepare the evening meal. This was life in and around the pueblo during the *Guerra Civil*, and in the long, long years of dictatorship that followed it.

CHAPTER 15

EL CAMINO DE FRANCIA
(The road to France)

In the late 1960's, the growing rise of living standards in the urban areas of Spain was not reflected in the rural ones, where there was still little development and where poverty and shortages were not mitigated. The regime combined the loosening of the economy with a tightening of political controls which, although resisted in the towns by the growing middle classes, worsened conditions in the countryside.

In Sedella, as in most other small villages, this resulted in an exodus from the pueblo. Many left to work in the large towns, such as Madrid and Barcelona, whilst more went to European countries, especially to Germany and Switzerland in the case of Sedella. Here they would, and still do, spend several years working, only coming back for a few weeks each year, before finally returning home. Our neighbour, Salva, lived and worked for six years in Switzerland, whilst his wife remained in the village with their children. This semi-exodus of many of the village men brought cash back to the pueblo, a much needed and scarce commodity, as there was no local employment at all.

Some others left the country to go to the New World, the Americas, perhaps never to return.

In Sedella, several pairs of goatherds used to breed large flocks of goats to walk along the *cañadas,* drovers' roads, from the village to the French border, in order to sell the meat to French butchers. This story has been put together using some snippets of information given to me by two of them, Salva and Fraquito, with a slice of imagination around them.

Salva was in his late forties when he made the first trip in 1969. As a teenager, he had fought in the last days of the battle of Madrid, when it fell to the Nationalist forces in 1939. When I asked him on which side he had fought, he simply looked at me and said "For

Franco, of course." It was a stupid question to ask, as in February 1937 Málaga fell to the Nationalists, and the pueblo was taken by them shortly after that. Any youngster in the village had then no option than to join their army when conscripted, except that of trying to escape to Republican held territory and thereby risk execution.

Fraquito's family were millers and owned one of the two flour mills which were within the village (there was a larger mill on a hillside a short distance from the pueblo). When I visited him to talk about his experiences on the walk, he showed me round his home where he then lived alone in his old age. The house was literally built around the milling equipment which was then still in place. A leather drive belt ran from the upper floor, which was one open area, to the lower. On the top floor were two beds, still made up, one of which had belonged to his parents and the other to his grandparents. On the ground floor, there were two sets of stone grinding wheels, some lifting gear and a bread oven. The whole of the lower floor was divided into two rooms (with half the milling equipment in each room), with a small bathroom that had been added fairly recently. The family used to live around this machinery even when it was in use.

Both men were literate; Fraquito often sat outside his house in the sun, reading a variety of books and magazines. This says a lot for the policies of Primo de Rivera in the 1920's. Primo was a 'benevolent dictator' in the eyes of many people, he led an army coup which put an end to several years of unrest. During his years in office, he made an alliance with the socialist party led by Largo Caballero, who became a councillor of state. His government had an extensive programme of public works, established the *Banco Exterior de España* and several more semi-state banks, created new state industries, established a health service and improved beyond recognition the education system, building many new schools, especially in rural areas. His reign was eventually brought to an end because his iron rule stifled all political freedoms. The return of political chaos that followed was to produce, eventually, the Civil War and the rise of Franco, a different sort of dictator altogether. His rule, in contrast to that of Primo de Rivera, which was one of prosperity, brought a decline in living standards, public health and educational provision, and explains why when I arrived in the nineties, the very old were literate whilst most of the following generation were not.

Both men died many years ago, but not before telling me of aspects of their journeys. When Salva was describing to me the three trips they had made to France together with their goats, he said, "We sold enough milk each morning to buy bread, cheese and onions, enough to eat for the day, and perhaps some other things if they were available and we had enough money." After reaching France and then selling their goats, the men would travel back to the pueblo using *coches lineas*, long distance buses, and trains. Salva said that on their third and last trip they had flown back to Málaga from Bilbao via Madrid to save time, the fare being more than covered by the sale of their animals. What occurred to me was that whether coming back by train, bus or plane, I wouldn't have wanted to be sitting next to men who had spent months with their goats, had only washed in the rivers they crossed and had carried few or no spare clothes with them.

At the time of their first walk in 1969, there were not many privately owned cars in the rural areas, or in the country as a whole, and those who had them did not travel far from the towns. Although the route of the *cañada* sometimes ran at the side of the main road through Spain, there was very little traffic. I remember in the early 1970's travelling for miles on empty roads, the biggest problem being to locate petrol stations, which were few and far between.

A change was in the offing however, and in a little over ten years after their third journey in 1971, this road would become much busier, a new dual carriageway built over both it and the *cañada* beside which it ran. The disappearance of these long protected animal routes has now prohibited any more long distance herding of animals. When Salva was describing his experiences to me, he offered: "buy some goats and I will walk with you on the route we took, to show you how it was". This offer, well meant I've no doubt even if in jest, was negated by the disappearance of long stretches of the *cañada*s under roads, his age and my reluctance to become a goatherd.

◊   ◊   ◊   ◊   ◊

On Wednesday morning the day dawned clear and fine, and by half past six the sun was a red disc low on the eastern horizon. To the west, the serrated skyline of the *Sierra de Guadarrama* rose blackly in the dim early light. Around the two men the goats were beginning to stir, their bells sounding unnaturally loud in the still morning air. The sitting man, huddled in his *manta*, blanket, rose stiffly to his feet stretching and yawning, and kicked his sleeping companion stretched out on the ground beside him.

"Salva, wake up," he half grunted, rubbing a hand over the stubble on his jaw. Lifting his wine skin, he squirted a jet of raw red liquid into his open mouth, swilling it round and then swallowing. A warm glow spread through his body as he stirred the reluctant sleeper once more with his toe. The bulky shape of his friend, rolled up tightly in his *manta* against the night chill and early morning dew, stirred reluctantly and looked up.

"Fraquito, *hombre*," he muttered thickly, rolling over and climbing slowly to his feet, easing his aching muscles. He glanced around the flat landscape where the looming black outlines of walls and trees were beginning to take on colour in the increasing daylight.

"*Hombre*, it's going to be hot again today, and dry and dusty. This country, it's too flat and open for me, not like that around the pueblo."

"We'll have hills soon enough," Fraquito replied, pointing to the outline of the sierras, which were clearly visible in the distance, barring their route. The Guadarrama mountains had been to the left of their route for the last few days, slowly closing in from the west to eventually cross their path at the pass of the Somosierra, the highest barrier between Madrid and the north of Spain.

The two men had left Sedella on the morning of the 14th April in 1969, just over seven weeks ago, to begin a journey of over 1100 kilometres, taking their flock of nearly 200 goats to sell on the French border. It was now the 28th of May and they were slightly more than halfway to the markets near Irun.

A short distance from where they had spent the night was the pueblo of Gascones, towards which the two men now drove their goats. They left the *cañada,* and entered the village by means of a small dirt track and made their way to the *plaza*, village square. The pueblo was already awake, many labourers had by then left to work in the surrounding wheat fields. The two men from Sedella penned their flock into a corner and called out *leche, leche, leche fresca,* milk, fresh milk. Soon a group of black-clad women gathered round them, and Salva began milking the goats into the jugs the women had brought with them. "One litre", "two litres" and so on, the women ordered, handing over a few pesetas in return.

During the milking, Fraquito took some of the money and went into the bar in the square, returning with two cups of coffee and two glasses of *sol y sombre*, sun and shade, a mixture of brandy and *anis*. Both men drank the spirits and sipped at the hot coffee, feeling a warm glow spread and ease the aches and pains of the night and the previous day's walk. Fraquito then took some more of the pesetas from the sale of the milk and disappeared down a side street. He returned with fresh bread, some cheese and a couple of onions.

Once the milk had all been sold, the two men packed the food into their haversacks, which they carried over one shoulder when they walked, together with their water bottles and wine skin. After filling their flasks with water at the fount in the plaza, they herded the goats back down the narrow lane to the *cañada* and resumed the journey north. The route they were travelling through Spain, with a few exceptions such as when it traversed the outskirts of Madrid, went through the rural countryside where both food and money were scarce.

For most of the time since leaving Madrid, they had been walking on the *cañada real Segoviana,* the Royal Segovian drovers' road. A network of these *cañada*s existed at that time which covered the whole of the country and which was protected by statute, allowing the free movement of animals across the land. The whole walk of *el camino de Francia,* the way to France, would take them about three months to complete, and each night they would stop near to a pueblo or town on the route, selling the milk from the goats to buy their food for the journey. At Madrid, where they had stayed for two days to rest, they had sold off two of the flock that had turned lame, and used the money to pay for a corral for the animals and a bed in a *posada* for themselves. Normally when they stopped for the night, with the animals loose on the drovers' road, they had to sleep on the ground in turns, the other man staying awake to make sure the goats did not wander away and to protect them from predators.

In Sedella, both men kept herds of goats, and over the last year they had bred a large number of kids, nearly a hundred each, to take to France in the following spring.

Salva and Fraquito, by taking their goats to sell to the French, brought back to the village some much needed capital. There was little chance of selling any quantity of goat meat locally at that time due to a lack of cash locally. The milk tanker, which later came regularly to the pueblo to purchase milk from all the goatherds, had not at that time started running, and the only milk they could sell was to the villagers themselves. At the border however, the men could sell their animals for between 1000 and 2000 pesetas each, probably about 3500 Euros or so in today's money. Two hundred goats could at these prices bring each man the equivalent of about one and a half thousand pounds at current rates. This would have been a small fortune in a cash-starved rural economy with a low standard of living.

Before leaving the pueblo for their walk to France, the two men first had to journey to Vélez-Málaga several times, to acquire the necessary papers that would allow them to move their goats across the length of the country. The fact that they were literate allowed them to do this, but the mass of forms to be filled in, and the number of visits they had to make to the Ministry of Agriculture offices, took many weeks. These offices, like all government ones of the time, worked slowly and obstructively, long queues forming during the morning, and shutting for the day at 2 pm. Anyone not attended to by then had to return the next day and queue again. Eventually, however, the papers were obtained, the flocks ready, the weather set fair and on Monday 14th April, they left the pueblo early in the morning.

The first few kilometres took them to the nearby pueblo of Canillas de Aceituno. This was a well-known route that both often travelled. Before the construction of the new road a few years earlier, Salva had often gone to fiestas in Canillas using the mule track, and then returned home by the same route in the early hours of the morning. He preferred the girls in Canillas to the ones in the pueblo, anyway there he was not under the eyes of his parents. From Canillas, they travelled by a rough track down the shoulder of the hill to Alcaucín, where they stayed overnight. From here the next morning, they followed a track which runs along the contours above the *río de Alcaucín*, and then climbs up to the pass through the sierras at *Ventas de Zafarraya*.

Once through the pass, the hills of the Axarquía were left behind, and they walked for many days over the flat meseta of central Spain, by way of Jaén and Bailén to Madrid. At first, the tracks and *cañadas* passed through olive farms, and then around Valdepeñas through the extensive vineyards of that area, before entering the grain fields of the central plain. They had reached Madrid on the evening of Monday the 19th of May.

After leaving Madrid on the following Thursday morning, they travelled for five more days before arriving at the *aldea*, hamlet, of Fuente Blanquilla, the night before their arrival at Gascones. Because the *aldea* was so small, just a cluster of four or five houses, they had not been able to sell all their milk or buy much food. The route to Gascones from Fuente Blanquilla crossed the river Lozoya and the flooded marshy area around it, where the going was hard, and they had arrived in the evening tired and hungry. Before settling down for the night on the *cañada* outside Gascones, they were able to buy food and drink in the village.

In the morning, after they had resumed their journey northwards, it became, as Salva had predicted, very hot with the dry dusty airless quality of the arid meseta in summer. As it was towards the end of May, the wheat was almost fully grown, and labourers worked in the fields on both sides of the *cañada*, weeding and irrigating the crops. By midday, the countryside emptied and all activity stopped, as the workmen sought shelter and took their siesta out of the sun.

Salva and Fraquito halted too, sheltering under the shade of a tree to rest and eat, the goats grazing around them. Close to the *cañada* was the main road between Madrid and the north, which would now run by their side until both *caminos,* routes, the road and the *cañada*, crossed the sierras at the pass looming ahead. The only traffic on the road was an occasional lorry and a few buses. Long before the workmen returned to the fields, the two men set out again and were soon in the valley below the pass, with the mountains closing in from both sides. Far off behind and below them, two black spots appeared on the road beside which the *cañada* now ran. As they grew nearer, the two men could see that they were motorbikes driving side by side on the single track road.

The bikes came to a halt beside the flock of goats, their riders in green uniforms covered in grey dust dismounted and crossed the verge to the drovers' road.

"Where are you from? Where are your papers?" asked one of the Guardia Civil to the two shepherds. This was a perpetual question asked of them, sometimes two or three times a day as they walked, all the way along the route. Guardia patrols on foot, mule, motorbike, and even occasionally in a car, had stopped them, asking for their credentials. And every time they were stopped it was by two officers, always two. The Guardia never went out on patrol singly, a custom they have continued to follow since their inception in 1844, under the government of General Ramon Narvaéz, to the present day. Because of this practice of always patrolling in pairs, they are known by many as *los gemelos,* the twins.

Wearily, Salva and Fraquito produced their identity cards, and the papers which permitted them to take their animals out of Andalucía and through the provinces of Old and New Castilla, Navarra and Vizcaya. For half an hour, the two officers questioned the men from Sedella, before remounting their bikes and roaring up the nearby empty road in a cloud of dust.

Fraquito spat into the dust at the edge of the road. "*Adios,*" he said after the now distant riders. The two men and their animals then resumed their progress up the *cañada*. The road beside them was not busy, despite being one of the main routes through the country, with only commercial traffic and the occasional car.

As the afternoon wore on, the dusty margins at the side of road became busy with carts, mules and oxen. By the early evening, the men and their flock had reached the pueblo of Robregordo at the bottom of the long three kilometre climb up the hill to the *Puerto de Somosierra,* the pass at the end of the Guadarramas. Here they stopped for the night. Salva went into the village to buy some provisions with their remaining pesetas from the morning. Then, after eating and drinking some brandy, they settled down for the night, first one and then the other keeping watch through the hours of darkness.

The next morning was a repeat of the day before, and many more before that, with the men taking their flock into the *plaza* of the pueblo in the early morning and milking their goats, selling the milk, buying food and drink and then once more resuming their journey.

Then, throughout the early morning, they climbed the steeply rising slope of the pass, 640 metres in three kilometres. They reached the *posada* on the summit in mid morning, where they paused for a rest and some refreshment. Before them stretched the meseta of Old Castilla, flat with here and there high serrated hills rising out of it. It was a brown landscape with a patchwork of green areas, finally fading into a blue haze where sky and land merged in a shimmering horizon. Stretching through the middle was the road, running in an almost straight line due north, a black line growing ever thinner as it ran from where they stood into the distant indefinable horizon. Immediately below them, at the foot of the descent, the church tower of Cerro de Abajo was visible above the roofs of the village.

"That's our route, *amigo,*" said Salva, pointing along the line of the road. "And then just after Boceguillas, we bear off right and head for Logroño. After that we go to Pamplona, and then over the hills to Irun," he added, looking at the map he had taken from his haversack.

It would be another forty-two days before they reached Irun, and sold their flock to the French traders who came over to buy them. The papers they carried did not permit them to cross the border with their goats, and the custom was for the French butchers to come over and buy the animals in Spain. After selling their goats, they would then travel back to the pueblo using buses and trains.

This Thursday morning however, on the last day of May 1969, they spent an hour allowing their flock to rest and graze after the hard climb and looked with some apprehension at the vastness ahead of them, before once more resuming their Camino de Francia. The two

143

men were to make this walk twice more in the following years, but this was the first time either had been this far north before, and they gazed with awe at the spectacle of the vast plain spread out below them.

CHAPTER 16

LA MUERTE Y LA VIDA
(Death and life)

For five weeks towards the end of 1975, the whole of Spain waited in silent anticipation for the inevitable event, *la muerte,* the death, which was to change the course of the nation for ever. It was in fact to bring new life to the country, although at the time no one could predict exactly what would happen. Some waited in fear, hoping for no change at all, for the old ways set for over thirty tedious years to continue. Others waited in hope, praying that after the *muerte* would come a *vida nueva,* a new life, to bring to an end thirty-six years of oppressive rule by a vindictive, cruel and seemingly heartless dictator.

Franco was on his death bed, connected by a web of wires to a life support machine.

Bleep; bleep; bleep; bleep.

Day and night, night and day, for week after agonising week.

Many changes had of course already taken place during his reign, a limited press freedom was now allowed, but limited it certainly was. Industrialisation and tourism were slowly bringing a new prosperity to some of the populace, especially in the urban areas.

However, the Movement was still in control of the country, a movement created by the dictator out of the Falange, the Carlists (or royalists) and all the other right wing parties that had supported the Nationalist cause in the Civil War. Once in power after the war, Franco had disbanded all these parties by decree and combined them into the *Falange Español Tradicional* which he later renamed the *Movimiento Nacional,* National Movement.

Also, the bureaucratic and centralised form of government that he created still governed the country, making development and modernisation difficult to achieve, and allowing bribery and corruption to run riot. Many a traveller to Spain in the late 1960's and early 1970's, when tourism began to spread through the Costas, will

145

remember how long and tedious was even the simple process, elsewhere at least, of cashing a traveller's cheque.

Despite the passage of time since the end of the Civil War, there were still numerous political prisoners in the gaols and many others were in exile, unable to return to their own country. Still more were in hiding, afraid to come out into the open, one such in a village near to Málaga lived in a cupboard in his home, unknown to the rest of the town. In the pueblo itself, several fugitives lived in the open on the slopes of the Sierra Tejeda, supported by the inhabitants of the village but, in theory at least, without the knowledge of the authorities.

Ex-soldiers and war veterans from the Republican army, even if disabled, were not granted pensions or given any form of financial support. The state of these ageing veterans, and the refusal of Franco to countenance any form of financial assistance to them, led one disabled ex-major from his own army, a loyal supporter of his cause in the war, to angrily refuse his own pension, despite the poverty this action brought to himself.

Even after all this time since the end of hostilities, executions of 'terrorists' and others connected to the Republican cause still took place. Indeed, one such highly publicised execution of several of these so-called terrorists occurred only a few weeks before the final illness of the dictator. This event led to an outcry from the rest of the civilised world, and much diplomatic upheaval, including such measures as the withdrawal of ambassadors.

Although it was years since the end of the Civil War, large garrisons of the army were stationed outside all the major cities, ready if necessary to mobilise against any perceived threat to the regime, and the Guardia Civil still held the countryside in an iron grip. In the cities, Franco had created a new force, the *policia armada*, to mirror the civil guard of the countryside, who held the urban populace in an equally firm grip.

Now the whole country, Republican and Nationalist, exile and franquista, rich and poor, urban or country dweller, waited as the days passed, suspended in time, aware only of the regular and inevitable passage of that time as measured by the monitor.

Bleep; bleep; bleep; bleep; on and agonisingly on.

Some years previously, in 1973, Franco had handed over the presidency to Admiral Carrero Blanco, an old hard line Civil War ally of his. He handed over the presidency, but still retained in his own hands the ultimate power. Carrero was killed shortly after his elevation to president by an explosion engineered by Basque separatists, an event which provoked a crackdown and a resurgence of much of the anti-liberal policies that were being slowly relaxed at the time.

Arias Navarro, another hard line franquista, who had made his name as 'the butcher of Málaga' by his savage acts after the fall of that town to the Nationalist army in the Civil War, was then named by Franco as the new president.

1975 opened with a resurgence of violence from both the right and the left, worse than at any time since the end of the Civil War. Shortly after the executions, mentioned earlier, of the group of 'terrorists', Franco made what was to be his last public appearance. In this speech, Franco denounced all opposition to his regime and the Movement, and all the forces for change and liberalisation as being a conspiracy between 'freemasons, communists and other enemies of order'.

Against this background of struggle, oppression and the dead hand of control at all costs, were some signs of hope and change from at least one quarter of what had been part of the status quo. The Catholic Church, which had for years supported the regime and had, at one time, even thanked Franco for 'overthrowing the communist and other agents of anti -Christendom', and had bestowed on him the honour of 'Knight of the Order of Christ', was now changing rapidly. The Church in the Basque region had always supported the anti-Franco cause, being more concerned with national independence than with perceived communist threats, and by the early 1970's the Church in Spain at large was also becoming more opposed to his cause. The Spanish bishops issued an open letter asking for forgiveness for their support of the Nationalists in the Civil War, and the Pope was said to be on the verge of excommunicating Franco himself for his continuing policies of repression. Many of the bishops and younger clergy were, by the early 1970's, openly supporting the liberal cause. The older, more traditional and conservative priests,

147

especially in the countryside, were still however firmly wedded to the forces of reaction.

Industrialists and Trade Unionists alike were now united in their demands for more liberalisation of state and financial controls on their operations, and insisting on more political democracy to further and quicken the slow economic advances that were taking place. In the tourist centres and on the Costas, the waves of holidaymakers from the rest of Europe and America produced a constant pressure for reform. Finally, the growth of international television and cinema highlighted the possibilities that change could bring, and contrasted the lifestyles of Spain with that of the democratic nations. For years, Franco had used the television as an 'opium' for the populace, feeding them hours of football, bullfighting and game shows to stifle political debate, and now that very same medium, so encouraged by him, was fuelling the forces for change.

Now all was stilled, in abeyance, as all sides were seemingly mesmerised by the steady progression from here to....... where?

Bleep; bleep; bleep; bleep.

In the centre of these pressures for on the one hand the continuity of repression, and on the other hand for the possibility of change and liberalisation was, perhaps, the most unknown and enigmatic of all the various factors, Prince Juan Carlos.

Juan Carlos had been chosen by Franco to be the future King of Spain, when he declared that Spain was to be a Monarchist Presidential State in the future. Franco chose Juan Carlos over his father, Don Juan, the legitimate heir in exile. Franco made the young Prince swear to uphold the state and the Movement, and to ensure that the status quo was maintained. Juan Carlos, at his investiture as heir to the throne, for Spain was not to be allowed to actually have a King during Franco's lifetime, only a prince in waiting, swore allegiance to both Franco and the *Movimiento Nacional* whose leader he was supposed ultimately to become. For years, Juan Carlos had stood behind Franco on state and other occasions 'with a frozen, wooden expression on his face'. At the same time, it was rumoured that the Prince had secret meetings with liberal and even socialist leaders of the, theoretically, still outlawed opposition. At one time, he was told in no uncertain terms by Franco: "the choice is Your Highness's; you can either be a Prince or a private individual."

Who, at this time of tense anticipation could tell what sort of King the Prince would make? Who could predict that after the death of the dictator, the new leader in waiting would be the key figure in the changes ahead? Yet, shortly after the death of Franco, the feelings of the Prince were to become abundantly clear. Soon after he was invested as King, he would sack President Arias Navarro and replace him with Adolfo Suárez, who whilst being, inevitably, a member of the Movement would help the young King bring about the liberalisation of Spain. Within two years, together they were to abolish the Movement to which both had sworn loyalty, institute elections and dismantle nearly all of Franco's repressive measures. Trade unions and even the communist party would be legalised, exiles would be allowed to return, and a new constitution formed. Many of these reforms would be carried out by Suárez together with a young socialist lawyer, still at the time in exile, one Felipe Gonzales, destined to become Spain's first socialist President.

When, some years later, a new right wing coup was attempted by sections of the civil guard and the army, it would be the King himself who effectively put down the revolt by telephoning his generals and informing them that they would only succeed over his, literally, dead body. The coup then collapsed leaving the colonel of the civil guard, Tejero, who had seized parliament at gunpoint, stranded and alone. The King's action led to a senior supporter of the Republic, who had been its leader in exile, to say "we are all royalists now".

But in 1975, with Franco on his deathbed, these events were still in the doubtful and unknown future, the whole nation waiting in trepidation and suspense.

Bleep; bleep; bleep; bleep.

For days, everyone was glued to their radio sets whilst the doctors battled to keep the dictator alive, fearful to let him die. Tensions ran high, so much seemingly being dependent on the steady bleep of the monitor.

How could so much depend on the presence 'alive' of a, for the most part, unconscious and powerless figure, who was heard to mutter at one point that he did not realise how hard it was to die? The doctors however, one of whom was Franco's own son-in-law, strove to the end to keep his heart beating.

Bleep; bleep; bleep; bleep.

In the pueblo, tension and feelings also of course ran high, with the people grouped around radios in their homes and in the small bars, waiting for news. There were no television sets here as there were on the coast, even radios were frowned upon by the traditionally minded officials who controlled the village. Little liberalisation had reached this high up the steep-sided sierra, despite its nearness to the Costas below. It was years behind in any changes that were taking place nationally. On the coastal fringe below the pueblo, foreign tourists had brought a tide of change, more money and a more open way of life, but the tide did not wash this high up the hill, and no tourists ventured up the steep winding roads of the Sierra Tejeda. Even the road to the village had stopped at Canillas de Aceituno until the mid sixties, and there was still no road to Árchez. Sedella and nearby Salares were only accessible by mule tracks prior to the coming of the road to Sedella in the sixties, and that as yet did not go further than Salares.

The pueblo had suffered much during the 'hungry years' at the end of the Civil War. Along with much of the Axarquía, which had mainly supported the Republican side, they had had retribution heaped on them. At one point, the local villages had been instructed to send their flour down to Torre del Mar where it would be baked, and the bread then distributed, the pueblo getting a share back. The baker in the mill above the village had taken to doing two mills a day: a small one in the morning, the flour from which was then collected by the Guardia and taken to Torre, and a larger, second, secret one at night, which the villagers used. One woman, who was commanded by the Guardia to give them the bread from this secret bake, replied in no uncertain terms, telling them to clear off. She spent six months in gaol in Vélez-Málaga for her defiance, and was still living in the village when I first came here, an older but still formidable woman. Her daughter, who was as radical as her, was a leading light in the women's movement until her death a few years ago.

The reforming pressures at the heart of the church were not to be found here in the pueblo, where the local priest was of the old tradition and to this day viewed Franco as a saint and a saviour. The schoolteacher also taught the values of the old regime and condemned liberal and democratic pressures as unpatriotic. The postmaster was an old-time Falangist, and perhaps the worst of the three local officials. Supremely bureaucratic, keeping the queues in the post office long, and controlling the passage of letter and parcel to a slow trickle. Once, he had had a villager shot for taking a melon from his vegetable plot.

Life in the pueblo was hard and the 'hungry years' that had followed the Civil War had lasted longer here, indeed could still perhaps be said to exist. The small Guardia Civil force that was stationed in the village exercised an iron control over the inhabitants.

If the country as a whole could not predict the future, how could the people of the pueblo, backward and cut off as they were, tell what would happen?

Breath by breath over the last days of the dictator, the village hung suspended in time, waiting, but for what?

Perhaps the priest could sense the resentment of his congregation to his sermons, could feel the lack of interest and, by their glazed expressions, the way his audience stopped listening to him when he spoke. Perhaps he knew that they only came to the church for the sacraments, prayers and worship, and had long since blotted out his words.

The schoolteacher in the same way must have been aware of the contempt of his pupils and their parents. He may well have sensed that when his back was turned, as he wrote on the blackboard perhaps, that his pupils pulled faces and made gestures at him. Perhaps he heard them at play outside the school, and realised that he was the butt of their jokes, the enemy in their secret games.

Similarly, perhaps, the postmaster could feel the waves of contempt and silent mulish resentment from his customers and those he made to suffer with his petty rules and ignomies.

All three of them probably realised the hatred and contempt in which they were held. An attitude held by all but a very few of the villagers, those few who were broadly to the right politically, and who therefore held similar views to the three officials. The majority silently passed them by in the street with averted eyes. The sentiments of the villagers were also made plain by the silence that fell when one of them passed groups gossiping in the street.

The populace did not know which way the King would turn after Franco's death, did not know if the forces of reaction or reform would prevail, and certainly could not have anticipated the speed and extent of the liberalisation that followed. Yet despite this, within 24 hours of Franco's death, these three dignities, the priest, the schoolteacher, and the postmaster, had left the pueblo. Quickly and secretly they fled to places unknown, never to return or be heard of again.

So the country waited breath by breath.

Bleep; bleep; bleep; bleep.

Future king, future president Felipe Gonzales in exile in France, generals, bishops and populace alike. And in the pueblo, small groups gathered around their semi-illegal radios also waited.

Bleep; bleep; bleep; bleep..............

At 6 am on the morning of 20th November 1975 the end came, Franco was dead.

Bleep; Bleep; Bleep: ....

A goatherd, listening to a radio as he milked their flock in the early morning, together with his father and brother, heard the news with awe, wonder and a mounting excitement. They burst out into the street shouting the news, other people hearing the rumpus flocked outdoors and, learning the reason for the uproar, joined in the growing scenes of relief and joy. That day the pueblo, according to what the goatherd told me, held an impromptu and celebratory fiesta.

La muerte y la vida. Death and life.

CHAPTER 17

LOS CAMBIOS DESPUÉS DE FRANCO
(CHANGES AFTER FRANCO)

It was two years after the death of Franco before Adolfo Suárez, the new president, put in place by the King, abolished the Movement, legalised all the opposition parties and an election was called. In 1978, Felipe Gonzales and Suárez constructed a new constitution, a democratic monarchy, with an elected *Cortes,* parliament. Gonzalez, the socialist leader of the PSOE, was the first prime minister of this *Cortes.* It was not until then that the nation was reasonably sure that a new era had at last dawned, and the country began to change dramatically.

During the last few years of Franco's life, when his grip on power was beginning to weaken, pressures for change were growing but the status quo and the Falange were holding back any significant advances. It was a pressure cooker waiting to explode. The main forces pushing for reform were mostly external, such as the increasing influence of the USA; the expansion of industry, especially in Catalan and the Basque area; and the growth of tourism on the Costas. Franco, despite his opposition to capitalism and his therefore suspicion of America, had accepted their money and the presence of NATO troops in his country. America was encircling the USSR with missiles and wanted them on Spanish soil. Franco's hatred of communism was greater than that of capitalism, and he accepted both money and troops from the USA.

Despite these pressures, any progress was slow and resisted by the bureaucracy of the state and the Falange.

I remember whilst I was on holiday in Bilbao in 1973 how high fear and tensions were during a general strike in the region. Strikes were illegal, and the Guardia patrolled the streets in pairs, with sub machine guns at the ready in their hands. Several people were shot by them for minor offences. The whole town was a powder keg just waiting to explode, which fortunately didn't happen. I was at dinner one night in a Spanish friend's flat when her husband got a phone call. Shortly after, he left the flat after a brief word with her. I hadn't known that he was a senior manager in one of the steelworks and a secret supporter, perhaps even a member, of a Basque Nationalist party. One of his workforce had been arrested by the Guardia, and he had hurried off to see if he could help secure his release.

As a tourist I, like many others on holiday, did not realise the tense state of affairs in the country and the simmering resentments under the surface. The Costas were becoming even more popular with British and Northern European holidaymakers, who for the most part were blissfully ignorant of the ferment building up in the country. They saw the Guardia, as I did, patrolling the beaches, armed and sweating in their heavy uniforms, who sometimes prohibited topless bathers, but they noticed little else.

However, by 1978, the constitutional change had come and a new consensus arrived at by almost all the country, and change began in reality. There was only once after this that the 'old guard' tried to restore the dictatorship by another coup. Several generals devised a plot in 1981 to once again seize power and a group of Civil Guards, led by Colonel Tejero, seized the *Cortes* at gunpoint. This attempt failed as King Juan Carlos rang all of the military generals one by one and told them that the coup would only succeed 'over my dead body'. The generals all capitulated and Colonel Tejero was left alone in the *Cortes* chamber, and then he too surrendered. After this hiccup, the programme of change and reform slowly continued and Spain became, perhaps for the first time in its history, a safe normal democracy.

In the pueblo after 1978, changes also began to happen. The village was poor with little or no employment, with most of the inhabitants working in the *campo*. Slowly, money began to come into the village from a variety of sources, and with the money improvements were made. Some villagers, as they had been doing over the last few years, went to work abroad, to Switzerland, Germany and France, and sent money back to their families. The first mayor of the pueblo after the political changes was a communist and he, together with a local English estate agent, began to sell houses and plots in the *campo* to mainly British incomers. This put money into the pockets of the vendors, and employed locals to renovate village properties and build new homes in the countryside.

Another source of income to the village was that of grants for specific projects from the *Juntas* of Málaga and Andalucía, and from the EU. One of the PSOE mayors who followed the first communist one was especially expert at securing grants from outside sources for improvements to the village infrastructure.

The local shops also benefitted by the influx of *extranjeros,* foreigners, as did the *ayuntamiento,* town hall, with a flow of fees, rates and other charges. The locals in their turn began to renovate their own homes and the ayuntamiento to improve the *calles,* streets, etc with this income. It was a classic example of the Keynesian economic theory of the multiplier. Every peseta brought into the village was spent again and then again, resulting in an actual spend of perhaps two or three times the original value.

By the time I arrived in 1994, this programme of change was well under way and has continued until today.

◊   ◊   ◊   ◊   ◊

Emiliano was sitting in the seafood bar in Gatwick Airport, alongside his Estonian *novia,* girlfriend, eating a mixed seafood platter and drinking white wine. His *novia,* Marlene Molokova, sitting next to him, was also drinking white wine but she had a crab salad in front of her. Emiliano, Emi to his friends, was 45 years old and tall for a Spaniard at over six foot, with a balding head and slightly hunched shoulders. Marlene was of Russian parentage, black-haired with a willowy figure, and at only five four much shorter than him. They were travelling from London, where they both lived and worked, to Sedella in Spain, for the fiesta of San Anton. Their departure gate was not due to be displayed on the monitors for over an hour yet, so they were not rushing their lunch. Marlene was reading a book she had just bought, whilst Emi was sitting lost in thought.

Crowds of fellow travellers moved all around them, their voices rising and falling as they passed by. Emi had been speaking to his girlfriend, an Estonian, and two waiters at the bar, one from Moldova and the other an Italian, in English, and now found he was thinking in that language too. He was the senior engineer of a Spanish firm with its headquarters in Madrid. At present, he was head of their northern European branch presently situated in London. But who knows for how long? he thought, after Brexit. He had worked in Spain, Rumania, France and Morocco on a variety of projects for the firm. At the moment, his main building projects were a steel-framed high rise building, two motorway extensions and a large flood relief scheme. During his time working for the firm, he had been moving up the promotion ladder to his present position. He thought that he probably owed his seniority in the firm to his ability to speak five languages, as much as to his prowess as a civil engineer.

He was going back to the pueblo of his birth for a fiesta, as he usually did two or three times each year. When they got to the village, they would stay in the house that his mother had lived in, together with his brother, his wife and their two children who lived in Málaga. Since the death of his mother several years ago, he and his brother had kept possession of it, and both used it when they came back to the village.

Thinking of his mother took his mind back to his childhood growing up in the pueblo. He had been born in 1971, and was just four when the dictator Franco died. He couldn't really remember the dictatorship, and had only a vague memory of the joy that had spread through the village on news of Franco's death. He could remember the poverty of his early childhood however, the hunger and the way in which his mother and grandmother, his *madre* and *abuela* he thought, switching his thoughts back into Spanish, had slaved to keep the family finances afloat.

"I'm just going to look for something to buy for Mario's children." Marlene had finished her meal and interrupted his reminiscences.

"Okay," he replied and resumed eating. "Do you need any help?" Mario after all was his brother, and his children his nephews.

"No, I'll be a while so don't hurry. We've lots of time to kill." Nodding, he ordered himself another wine.

Thinking of those far off days of his childhood brought back many memories. The village had been in a poor state then, houses in want of care and attention, all the streets unpaved and the whole population, with few exceptions, poorly dressed and perpetually hungry. His *abuela*, like many of the older women in the village, was adept at creating meals from seemingly few ingredients. She was renowned for her stews made from scraps of pork or goat, *cerdo* and *chivo* he told himself, reverting once again to Spanish. But really, after weeks in England and surrounded by English speakers in the airport, it was easier to think in that language. Those bits of meat she had used as a base for the stews, together with some *morcilla,* black pudding, and *chorizo,* spicy sausage, augmented with vegetables from their own garden. Such as potatoes, leeks, cabbage, onions, carrots and so on, depending on what was in season.

He remembered how his mother had tried to paint the house each year, inside and out, with a coat of *cal,* now what was that in English? he pondered... ah yes, lime wash. If it wasn't done each year, it would peel off or discolour. Not like today when nearly everyone used modern plastic emulsions. Still white, of course.

When his brother was seven and he was five, his father had left home and gone to live in Málaga. He had seen little of him from then on until he was in his mid twenties and no longer living in the village. His father had been one of the few right wingers in the village, a supporter of the Falange, whilst his grandmother and mother were fervent socialists. They had got married, he realised much later in his life, because she had fallen pregnant with his brother, sex and mutual attraction having had little to do with politics.

He had never known his paternal grandparents or his maternal grandfather, all having been victims of the Civil War, as had one of his mother's brothers, and a brother and sister of his father.

He finished his meal, paid for both his and Marlene's, and went to look for her. He found her standing under the large board that displayed the gate numbers of all the flights from the north terminal. Their flight to Málaga was still fifteen minutes off being displayed. They went and sat together in the rows of seats nearby. She showed him what she had bought for his two nephews, a small teddy bear for

157

the baby boy, and a tee shirt for the older one. Then she went back to her book and he resumed his reminiscences.

When he was eight, the village school had reopened, and he had quickly learned enough to go on to the big school in Canillas when he was twelve. He was an intelligent boy and a quick learner, and he had then gone to university in Málaga and qualified as a civil engineer. During this time he had travelled to Málaga to study, and returned to the pueblo at weekends.

He remembered the day of the first free elections, when the PSOE had formed the government and the pueblo elected a communist mayor. He was an illiterate goatherd, but honest and ambitious for the village. Together with an Englishman who came to live in the village, he had begun the process of selling houses to foreigners, which was still going on today, though not in such great numbers since the clamp down on illegal building in the *campo*.

He got to know several of these British incomers quite well, and had gone to both England and Scotland to stay with them and their families during his early teens. It was on these visits that he had learnt English, and discovered his ability to learn foreign languages fairly quickly.

The village changed over these years too. The streets were mostly paved, even if only in concrete, houses were slowly improved, new bars were built and opened, and a football pitch developed over the new feria site. When he was eighteen his *abuela* had died, and he had got to know his father fairly well. By then, although his mother didn't want to have anything to do with her ex-husband, he was able to meet him and begin to form a reasonable relationship with him. The old enmities, though not gone, were now becoming less and, after all, they were father and son. His uncle Salva, his mother's elder brother, who had been forced to flee to Mexico during the Civil War, returned to the village in 1977, and he also met his father, and they came to some sort of mutual understanding, if not exactly friendship.

When he was twenty-three, after qualifying, he had left the pueblo to work for the civil engineering firm in Madrid, the one he was now a senior member of.

Here his thoughts were interrupted by Marlene telling him that their gate number was now on the board, and they both left the main area to start the process of boarding.

Once on the plane and with her once again reading her book, he thought of all that had happened since then: of the continuing improvements to the village infrastructure; the death of his mother, father and his *tío,* uncle, Salva. Then came the marriage of his brother, shortly after the death of their mother. This was followed by the birth of his two nephews. During all this time he had had a succession of *novias.*

As the plane passed over France and headed towards Spain and Málaga, he realised that his life too was moving on. Like his pueblo which had changed over his lifetime, both would continue to grow and develop. But perhaps now was the time for him to settle down somewhere. England perhaps, if that would still be possible after the Brexit vote, but if not then wherever his company relocated and sent him. Marlene had just told him that she was pregnant, so he had to come to a decision soon. She wanted to keep the baby and so, he realised, did he. After the sudden shock of her announcement, he realised that he wanted a family, like his brother. After all, he was now 45 and Marlene at thirty was, he realised, not just the latest of his *novias,* but the one he didn't want to lose.

He and Marlene would settle down and then, like his brother, he would bring their children back to the pueblo once or twice a year. They would go to Estonia too, and they would become Europeans in the true sense, live in one place but also have roots in two more, and above all, like him, his children would be *Sedellanos.*

Tonight in Bar Chiringuito, he would propose to Marlene and then celebrate with his brother and his wife, and whatever friends were in the village. For all his friends, if they hadn't stayed in the pueblo, returned for most of the fiestas, just like he did.

CHAPTER 18

LA FIESTA DE SAN ANTON
(The fiesta of San Anton)

The following three stories are of three differing fiestas I went to during my first couple of years in the village. They still take place and have altered or evolved over the years, but are substantially the same. Two others have been added, the first the *Romería* which I briefly mention when describing the Summer Fiesta, and the *Día de la Trilla*. This latter is held in the summer to celebrate the threshing of corn. A lot of the local pueblos have a day relating to crops, produce or the like. For instance there are fiestas of wine, *morcilla,* black pudding, *ajo blanco,* garlic soup, *nísperos,* kumquats, and many more. The pueblo also has events at carnival, culture week and on the Day of the Three Kings. The Spanish give their gifts not at Christmas but at *Día de Reyes,* Epiphany. In the village, the three kings ride in on mules, resplendent in costumes, and parade through the streets led by the town band, throwing sweets to the children. The procession ends up at the *salón* where presents are handed out.

So here is one of my first San Antons in the pueblo.

◊　◊　◊　◊　◊

The town band is at the front of the procession, its music echoing through the narrow streets of the pueblo, threaded by the wind which funnels through them. Following the band comes the float, carried by about ten men, on which rides the statue of San Anton Abad, St. Anthony Abbot, the village saint.

Somewhere ahead of the float are two of the *mayordomos,* organisers, of the fiesta, who pause every so often to fire off rockets marking the route of the procession.

Following the float, packed tightly into the narrow streets, are almost all the population of the village, augmented by visiting relatives and friends who swell the population over fiesta weekends. A long straggling snake winding through the village, from which rises

160

muted chatter punctuated by occasional shouts and laughter. As is normal at fiesta virtually everyone turns out, babies in prams, young children, teenagers, middle and old aged alike; all manner and types of people, including the holy and the profane, believer and non-believer, men, women, rich and poor, all united in returning the saint to his resting place in the *Ermita de Esperanza,* a small ancient chapel on the eastern fringe of the village.

It is Sunday evening and almost the final act of the weekend fiesta, all that remains after the statue is returned to its resting place is more music and dancing in the square in front of the church. It is from this *plaza* on the other side of the village that the procession had started, gathering there and then wheeling to the right down a narrow steep alley, punctuated at irregular intervals by steps of varying height.

I am walking next to Pepe Alegría, resplendent as always at fiesta in a smart grey suit, plum-coloured waistcoat and his wide-brimmed grey caballero or Córdoba hat. Next to us stumbles Pepe Molinero, slightly paunchy and balding, dressed casually in trousers and a woollen jacket. Also with us is Salva Redondo, soberly dressed and leaning heavily on a stick, and two others, still in working clothes having just returned from a day's work in the *campo.* We are behind Aurelia, with her youngest in a pushchair. Rafa, her husband, is one of the float carriers up ahead, whilst Carlos, her eldest son, is playing in the band. Next to her walks Ani, her sister, with her own son Alejandro. Ani's husband, also Rafa, is working in one of the village bars. My own wife is playing in the band, and so I join the procession with whatever friend I have been standing with in the square.

However, those around me are constantly changing as the street widens and narrows at corners, small squares and junctions. Now, only three or four can walk abreast and then, for a while, six or more is possible. At each junction, more people join the procession, so gradually it grows longer and longer.

Soon Pepe and I are walking behind a family I do not recognise, who are from outside the village, and next to Rafa Redondo, Salva's brother, from whom we bought one of our mules. In front of us are Adorín and Antonio, one of whose children is also playing in the band. There are only a few other *extranjeros*, foreigners, in the procession, most of them stand at junctions to watch it pass, or go straight to the end of the route to wait for its arrival.

We progress slowly through the village, with many stops as the float carriers up ahead take a rest, by stopping and putting the float down on to its stands. These stands are two metre long poles with metal cups, into which the float's arms fit. These poles are carried by a group of village children; there is also a longer pole with a metal cup on top, carried by one of the *mayordomos*, who uses it to lift low electricity wires so that the float can safely pass underneath.

The band will also cease playing from time to time, but when it does so Jorge on the trap drum still maintains a steady beat.

The fiesta started on Saturday when, in the morning, the streets were strung with small flags and lights. At midday, the church bells had been rung, and rockets fired off from in front of the church to declare the start of proceedings. In the late afternoon, the band had assembled in the square, and then went on a *pasacalle*. That is, they marched all round the village playing pasodobles, marches and other tunes. Also in the late afternoon, there had been a children's event in the *salón*, village hall. This year it was a trio of clowns who had given a performance. Later in the evening, the statue of San Anton had been brought in procession from the *Ermita* to the church, almost a mirror image of the one now taking it back. As with the procession tonight, it was escorted by all the populace and the visitors to the village. At midnight in the square, a group had played music on a stage especially erected for the occasion, and there had been dancing through to the early hours.

Sunday, however, is the main day of the San Anton fiesta. This year, the morning started with a display of *'Panda de Verdiales'* by a group from a nearby village. These are dancers in traditional dress led by either guitars, violins or both, and with a leader who is similar to the fool in English Morris dancing. As both *Panda de Verdiales* and Morris (Moorish) dancing have a common root, the similarities are obvious and observable.

Central to the fiesta of San Anton is the mass at midday, and the 'benediction of all the animals' that follows it. This event is usually referred to in shorthand as the 'mule blessing'.

St. Anthony Abbot was born in Egypt in 250 AD, and died in 356 AD at the ripe old age of 106. He was an Egyptian who inherited considerable wealth from his parents. One day, he had listened to a preacher on the text 'go sell all you have and give it to the poor'. He was converted and had done just that, only keeping a small sum back to educate his younger sister. He gave away the remainder of his wealth and became a hermit. He then brought together several other hermits and formed the first known monastic community. During his lifetime he was tempted many times to return to the world, some of those temptations brought about by a desire to own for himself various animals. When faced by such temptations, he got into the habit of blessing the animal before refuting the temptation. In this way he has become, for many Axarquían villages at least, the patron saint of animals, patron of the animal blessing fiestas. San Anton is the village saint of Sedella.

Traditionally in Sedella, all the village animals of goats, sheep, oxen, horses, mules and so on, were brought to the square in front of the church, to be blessed and sprinkled with holy water by the priest after the mass. Gerald Brennan, in his book 'South from Granada', which is an account of his life in a small village in the Alpujarras just to the east of Sedella, describes just such an event. However, the blessing of the animals in Yegen, Brennan's village, took place in April on St. Mark's day, not as here when it is held in January, on the nearest weekend to St. Anthony's day.

Nowadays in Sedella it is only the mules, horses and donkeys that are brought to be blessed. Whilst the village has many mules, used for working the land, it has only a few horses and donkeys. It became therefore mostly mules which were brought for blessing, hence the name 'mule blessing'. More recently small animals, dogs and pets, are also being brought to be blessed. This is due in part to the increase in foreign residents, and the increasing keeping of pets by the Spanish. At this fiesta, however, that change was several years away and so it was only large animals that were in the square.

All Sunday morning, the animals had begun gradually to appear on the streets, their riders going from bar to bar drinking in the saddle. Shortly before the end of the mass, the square filled with animals and riders jostling to be at the front, to be the first to be blessed. When the mass is finished, signalled by the firing of rockets in front of the church, the priest emerges accompanied by two attendant boys in surplices, and walks to the front of the raised area above the square. After a short prayer, he blesses the animals and throws holy water over both them and their riders, as they are continually brought forward for the benediction.

After being sanctified, each rider turns his mount and forces a way through the mass of animals waiting their turn, and out of the square. Once out of the square, they then form up in the street leading into it, facing the church. The float of San Anton is then brought out of the church down the steps and into the *plaza*. A procession then parades round the streets. In front, the inevitable mayordomos, firing off rockets every few yards, followed by the priest and two young altar boys. Then comes the statue on its *paso,* float, the band, as many villagers who want to join in, and bringing up the rear the mules, horses, and a couple of donkeys, that have been blessed. This procession winds through the pueblo to the *Ermita,* and then back by a different route to the church. Once back, the statue is returned inside and the procession dispersed. The animals and riders then ride round and round the village most of the afternoon via the bars, until those left at the end are less in control of the route than their animals. Slowly, the animals disappear off the streets and back to their stables, until by early evening only a few are to be seen tethered outside one or another of the bars.

Sometimes an *extranjero*, usually one who knows little if anything about horses, will complain of the danger of the animals 'racing through the narrow streets', or about the cruelty or the mess made by the dung on the streets. As someone who has been to the Appleby horse fair in Westmoreland, and witnessed the horses racing through the crowds there, I know that the danger levels at San Anton simply do not compare and most of the animals, apart from one or two of the horses, are not capable of speeding anywhere. There is little or no cruelty, these are working animals and as such, with a few exceptions, are well looked after and cared for. As for the dung, well animals do leave dung behind but this is cleaned up later in the day as Sedella, like most Spanish towns and villages, is kept well cleansed of litter and rubbish.

The fiesta takes place in January, and so it is usually dry, fine and warm by day and chilly overnight. Two years ago, however, it was unseasonably wet, with very heavy rain for all of the Sunday. The result was that no animals were brought to the church. At the end of the mass, the priest called from inside, "Are there any animals out there?" There happened to be an Alsatian dog outside at the time, with its owner. "Only a dog," came the answer. "Good enough," called the priest. However, the dog was just then scared by the rockets set off next to it, and its owner took it away. By the time the priest emerged, the square was empty of animals. In full vestments, under a large striped golf umbrella, he looked vainly around. The day was saved by José, slightly inebriated, leading his two mules up to the square from their stable nearby, in the downpour, to receive the blessing.

And now it is Sunday evening, and the procession is winding its way through the steep and crooked streets to the *Ermita*. Eventually it reaches the wide road opposite the school, just below the small hill on which the *Ermita* stands. The band then moves to one side and forms up facing the statue, which is placed on its rests. The crowd push into the small area and stand expectant.

Suddenly one, two, three rockets shoot up into the sky. These are not the processional rockets that simply explode, but display ones that burst into coloured showers and fall crackling and sparking over our heads. The firework display has begun.

Rockets, roman candles of many kinds, mortars and various types of fountains shoot upwards; Catherine wheels which turn into candelabras of roman candles, and then end in fiery exploding volcanoes; set pieces of many types all provide a spectacular display. At one point, there is a display which reads 'San Anton Sedella', that burns in red and yellow for a few minutes. Now, a continuous stream of yellow balls of fire whistle and scream as they race into the sky. All the time, mortars and rockets fly upward and explode over our heads. The crowd watch enthralled with many 'ooohs' and 'aaahs' and the band play tune after tune to accompany the display.

Suddenly it's all over with a series of even louder bangs, with showers of sparks let off from a row of boxes set off at ground level. The crowd around me relax, chatter and laugh, and then a wave of clapping sweeps across the square.

The statue is once more lifted and carried the last few yards, to a cobbled area just outside the chapel entrance. The band follows, playing as they go. The saint is raised above the heads of the bearers who, with arms outstretched, turn it round and round with cries of 'Viva'. At last the band plays the *Himno Nacional,* National anthem, and the float disappears through the door of the chapel, the crowd clapping all the while. Many of the followers crowd into the *Ermita* to see the float placed back into position. Once more, San Anton is back at rest in the *Ermita*, where he will stay for another year.

The crowd now streams back to the town square where the music group begin another performance. This year, as in many others, it is 'Orquesta Andalus', who play for about one and a half hours. The square fills and empties during this time, as people visit the bars and some go home to eat, but always there are couples dancing to the music, and towards the end of the performance, the square fills with anticipation for the flamenco singer.

At the end of their performance, Orquesta Andalus vacate the stage, and the flamenco singer and his guitarist take their places. Here in southern Spain, whilst there are displays of flamenco dancing, it is the singers that most Spaniards value.

The guitarist begins his warm up, slowly increasing his tempo, whilst the singer sits beside him, clapping to the rhythm and calling out encouragement from time to time. "Antonio .... Tonio .... *olé,*" until he is satisfied. Then the singer breaks into song. His voice ranges over several octaves, rising and falling in volume, and with a variety of speeds. The sound echoes through the square with the guitar always leading, but subservient to the voice. As the tempo rises *'olé'* rings out from the crowd, some of whom are clapping out the complex rhythm. At the end of each song the singer leaps to his feet, his voice seeming to go on and on without breath for minutes, and finishes with a loud final chord, stamping his feet. The atmosphere is electric, the crowd shouting encouragement during and at the end of each tune.

He sings *sevillianas*, *malagueñas* and *fandangos*, on and on, for over an hour. At the end, both performers bow and leave the stage, only to be called back for an encore.

Then the main group, Orquesta Andalus, return to begin their last performance. They will now play through to the early hours, when at 6 am the fiesta is concluded by a *'Gran Traca',* a continuous volley of loud fireworks fired off in a line.

The fiesta is over for another year.

CHAPTER 19

SEMANA SANTA
(Holy Week)

When we first came to Sedella, the holy week celebrations in the village were a bit low key. There was the silent Good Friday procession round the Stations of the Cross, but little at all on the Thursday. This has all altered now of course. Now we have our own *Cofradía,* and the band leads the two floats, one of Jesus with his cross and the other the Virgin, to the Calvary on the hill above the *Ermita* and back to the church. In our first few years, the band usually had a contract to play in the Vélez-Málaga parades on several nights, Thursday included. On our second Easter here, I think it was, I went down to Vélez with Frasco Miguel in his lorry to see them. Wendy was playing with the band and was already there. Frasco was a goatherd and regularly took his goats past our finca, so we got to know him quite well. Frasco is pronounced Fraco locally, as in this part of Spain an 's' in the middle or at the end of a word is usually not pronounced. People from other parts of Spain are easily spotted as they use the 's' in such words. In the story of our visit to Vélez that night, I will spell it Fraco to add authenticity.

◊　◊　◊　◊　◊

Fraco Miguel and I stood on a corner in the maze of narrow side streets that run up the side of the hill in Vélez-Málaga, from the fountain in the *Plaza Reyes Católicos,* the square of the Catholic Kings, which is at the end of the *Paseo de Andalucía,* (Andalucían Walk, I suppose we would call it) to the *Fortaleza,* Moorish castle, above. It was 10.30 pm on the evening of Maundy Thursday in *Semana Santa,* holy week. Round about us throngs of people passed by going in all directions, and echoing through the streets could be heard the steady and almost unearthly beat of a lone drum.

Then, through the night came the shrill tone and the dramatic beating of a cornet and drum band. Fraco looked at me and shook his head.

"That's not the Sedella band," he said.

"No," I replied, for I too could distinguish a cornet and drum band from a conventional wind one.

Fraco, however, had not waited for an answer but had charged off uphill. "This way," he called back. "I know where they are."

What he based this on, neither of us having a programme of the various routes of the parades, I did not know, but I had little option but to follow his lead or lose him in the crowds and the confusing lanes of Vélez. We arrived near the *Plaza San Juan de Dios,* the square of St. John of God, through which all the various parades pass at some time on their route. From near our new vantage point, we could hear the music of a wind band playing nearby.

"That's it," he cried and raced on through the crowds. When we turned the corner however, I could see that this was in fact a different band, that from Canillas de Aceituno, whose conductor I recognised.

Now we had trouble moving, for not only were the crowds thick on the narrow pavements on either side of the street, but the whole of the road between them was taken up with the procession. In front of us was a large float brightly lit by candles, on which rode the statue of the Virgin, carried by about 100 men. Filling the road in front of the statue were two lines of the members of the *Cofradía,* or brotherhood, in their tall pointed hats and long black robes, behind them was the band itself and behind the float two lines of women, in black dresses and tall majestic *mantillas.* Following them came the lines of penitents, in normal clothes, carrying candles, some walking barefoot. In the distance were the lights of a second float, on which rode the crucified Christ, behind which was the cornet and drum band we had heard earlier, or one like it. Further away still there would be, we knew, yet more members of the *Cofradía* and more penitents, who were out of our sight at the minute. The whole procession was moving slowly up the hill, swaying rhythmically from side to side, as it went towards the *Plaza San Juan de Dios*, which we had just left.

169

Undaunted by his mistake, Fraco turned and fought his way up the side street we had just come down, which had already filled up with spectators who had followed us, until the sounds of the band were almost lost amongst the baffle of the tall buildings of the *barrio.* Only a hollow echo of music and the dramatic dull beat of the drums were still audible to us.

As we turned a corner into a different street, the clear sounds of a different band came echoing down yet another side street.

"That's it," said Fraco, with just as much certainty as before. Given that this evening there were five different processions in the streets, most with two bands, what he based this conviction on was unclear to me. Yet as I listened, something about the tone, the mixture of instruments, seemed familiar. I nodded my head towards the space where Fraco had been standing to agree with him. Fraco himself however was already yards away, unheeding and unhearing, once again striding quickly in the direction of the sound.

This time he was right, it was the band of our pueblo, playing for the brotherhood who had hired them. We came upon them near a tight right hand bend where the bearers of the float, just in front of the band, were having trouble manoeuvring it round the corner, having to mount the pavements on both sides of the street and angle it past the walls on either side. There were also electric cables low overhead, which were being raised by a penitent using the long pole carried especially for this purpose.

Soon we were chatting to members of the band, as they took a break between playing marches, and with the small group of villagers from Sedella who were walking round Vélez with the band.

Fraco and I had travelled down to Vélez earlier that evening in his lorry which he, being one of Sedella's goatherds, normally uses for transporting goats and animal feed. On the side of the lorry was his name, Antonio Peña Bermudez, Fraco Miguel not being his actual name, just one he had assumed in his youth and by which he preferred to be known. Sometimes, when in conversation with Fraco and an older member of the village, or one of his relatives, who have known him since childhood, there seems to be one more member in

170

the group than reality, as he is addressed as Antonio by some and Fraco by others.

Fraco is a special friend of ours, he had in fact lived for about a year in the house we now own, and had given us the loan of his lorry, with himself as driver, on two occasions. Once he had transported our almond crop to Vélez to be sold, as that year we had a bumper crop and could not carry them down in our car. On another occasion, he had brought some building materials up the hill for us.

Tonight however we had come to Vélez together, Wendy who plays in the band having driven down earlier in our car. Fraco and I had arrived in Vélez at about 9 pm, and started the evening in a fish restaurant where we shared plates of *rosada,* a white fish similar to cod; *calamares*, not the bright rubbery rings served in the tourist centres of the Costas, but succulent young squid; and fresh local sardines. Whilst we were eating, we had watched the processions on the television in the restaurant, and had in fact seen our town band on it. Most towns in Spain have their own local television station, and Vélez-Málaga is no exception. That evening, Vélez TV was filming the processions live from five or six cameras placed around the town. The Sedella band was easily recognisable, the burly figure of Manolo, its director, at its head and then eight lines of four instrumentalists behind him. In the front the percussion section, drumming out the continuous and tingling regular beat of the slow march. Next came the trumpets, saxophones, trombones, tubes and French horns, with the clarinets, requintos and flutes bringing up the rear.

During *Semana Santa* there are many processions in Vélez, all being organised by the various *Cofradías* of the town. Every *Cofradía* has its own *paso,* float, most in fact having two. Each float carries a statue or image, depicting some aspect of the Easter story, including the Virgin or Christ himself. These floats are carried by between 80 to 100 men, members of the *Cofradía*. As the float moves along the route, it is swayed from side to side by its bearers, moving to the beat of the solitary drum which follows it, keeping up a regular rat-a-tat rhythm all the time. These *pasos* are attended by other members of the *Cofradía,* who wear the slightly sinister long robes and hooded cowls with tall pointed helmets. These helmets originate from the

171

times of the Inquisition, being worn originally by the prosecutors to avoid recognition. The pointed hats of the Ku Klux Klan also have the same origin. These penitents form up in two lines behind or in front of the *paso*. Most of them also have women attendants who wear black dresses and lace gloves, with *mantillas* and veils on their heads. Behind these, the families and supporters of the *Cofradías* also form up in two long lines carrying candles. The whole procession sways from side to side in time with the drumbeat and the float as it passes through the streets. A *Cofradía* with two floats, two bands and its attendants and supporters will take up several hundred metres of streets as they weave slowly round their route, crisscrossing each other in numerous places.

There are 18 *Cofradías* in Vélez-Málaga in total, giving a staggering number of people involved in the holy week activities, probably nearly half the adult population. Each float is spectacular with its statue, blazing candle light, intricate decorations and flowers. The cost to the members of the *Cofradías,* who rival each other in their presentation, must be immense. Each *Cofradía* owes its origin to a medieval guild, or is based on a group or trade in the area, or perhaps is rooted in a local *barrio,* area, of the town. The oldest *Cofradía* in Vélez is the *Real Cofradía del Santo Sepulcro,* Royal Brotherhood of the Sacred Sepulchre, which was founded in 1608. This brotherhood traditionally parades on the night of Good Friday.

Although not as famous or as large as the celebrations in Málaga, Granada or, perhaps the most well known of all, Sevilla, (where there are over 60 *Cofradías*) the ones in Vélez are just as spectacular and certainly more accessible for viewing, as the crowds watching are correspondingly smaller.

Of the 18 *Cofradías* in Vélez, one parades during the daytime on Palm Sunday and one during the daytime on Easter Sunday. Both of these are brotherhoods devoted to, in the first case, 'Jesus' triumphal entry into Jerusalem' and, in the second, 'His triumphant and glorious resurrection', phrases which form part of their names. All the other parades take place during the night time between Tuesday and Good Friday. On Tuesday, only two *Cofradías* have processions, whilst by Friday there are six. Each one starts at some point during the evening from 7 to 11 pm, lasting for about 5 hours, some therefore not finishing until 4 or 5 in the morning. Whilst they all start and finish at different places, they will pass through the *Plaza de San Juan de Dios*, from where they make their way up to the *Plaza de los Carmelitas,* the Carmelite square, where they pass in front of the Carmelite Monastery. Each *Cofradía* has a long and complicated title, tonight for example the band of Sedella are playing for the *Real Cofradía de Nuestro Padre Jesus del Gran Poder en su Tercera Caída y María Santísima de la Amargura* which translated means the 'Royal Brotherhood of Our Father Jesus of the Great Power on His Third Fall and the Most Holy Mary of Grief'.

It is hard to fully explain the emotions that the holy week parades arouse: the suspense and excitement of the crowds; the awe inspiring spectacle of the hooded figures; the elegant señoras in their *mantillas*; the magnificent and sombre floats; the dramatic cornet and drum bands and the sombre march music of the wind bands; and, perhaps especially, the eerie constant echoing drum beats that can be heard on all sides throughout the long night. The whole event can bring a tingle to the base of your spine, affect both pulse and heartbeat, and bring a feeling of apprehensive exhilaration.

Fraco and I now went ahead of the procession which included the Sedella band as it made its slow way to the *Plaza de San Juan de Dios,* where a very complicated manoeuvre takes place. When we reached the square, the first statue of the Virgin had already arrived, and was stood with its back to the church of *San Juan de Dios*, facing a small balcony on the house opposite on which several people waited. The cornet and drum band that had preceded the *paso* of the Virgin was formed up in a side road facing the square. This band was resplendent in red tunics and brass helmets, and had a white husky dog as its mascot. There was also a young boy of about 10, who was dressed identically to the band and who carried a cornet. The square, already full of spectators all round the edge, was now slowly overfilling with the attendants and penitents associated with the procession. Soon the second float, of Christ, arrived and forced its way into the square, whilst the band of Sedella formed up, blocking yet another road into the area.

Then first one statue and later the second was brought before the group on the balcony. This required much backing and moving forwards and sideways of the floats. During the change from first the Virgin and then Jesus facing the balcony, there was a period when each advanced towards the other and then backed off again, a manoeuvre repeated several times. During this process, I heard one English voice from the watchers complain that "it was a bit of a mess" and "needed better organising", not seeming to realise that the movements were in fact an organised and well-practised part of the event.

During the time that each float stayed facing the balcony, a time of perhaps ten minutes, a man and then a woman sang impromptu and unaccompanied *saetas,* sacred songs in the flamenco style, to the statue. The crowd responded with *"olé"* as each *saeta* reached a climax. A *saeta* to Christ may be on the lines of:-

"You who carry my soul
in your hands, O man of Nazareth
Ay! but who will be your consoler
and who will wipe away the sweat from your head."

One to the Virgin may similarly be on the lines of:-

"There can be no suffering like yours
no pain that is so intense as yours
no pain like that which pierces
and goes to the heart of the mother."

Each *saeta* is usually of four line verses, many of them sung to mother and son alike. They are mixes of praises and laments, with the Moorish influence of their derivation quite clear.

Between each group of *saetas,* during the manoeuvrings of the floats, first one band and then the other filled the square with music, the boy at the head of the cornet band playing some solos. At the end of the second set of *saetas,* a group of spectators, who had been on a balcony at roof level on the church opposite, lit a line of hand-held fireworks, each a fountain of yellow sparks which fell on to the heads of the crowd below, causing much amusement and a little consternation.

Then the procession slowly reformed and worked its way out of the square and moved off slowly down the hill, in the direction of the *Plaza Reyes Católicos* some way away at the bottom.

Fraco and I also left the square and made our own way more quickly down to this point, where another procession was at the time passing through the *plaza*, turning behind the fountain in its centre and then moving up the road towards the Carmelite Monastery. It was now about 12.30 am and Fraco said that it was time to go, as he had to be up at about 5.30 am to milk his goats.

"Right," I agreed, as I knew it would be at least an hour in his lorry back to Sedella.

"First though," he said, "let's walk up to the Carmelite Monastery to see the parade pass the stand."

So we walked up the hill, alongside the procession making its slow way up the road beside us. We reached the square at the top which was already full of spectators, many of them sitting at the side of the road on the rows of chairs that can be hired for the occasion. In front of the Monastery was the stand itself full of local dignitaries. We stood and watched as a *paso* reached the square and rested there. Here more *saetas* were sung in honour of the Virgin on the float. "*Olé*" rang round the square at the completion of every four line tribute.

By the time we had seen a second *paso* come into and leave the square, time was once more on Fraco's mind.

"We must go," he repeated.

"Yes, come on," I agreed. "It's up to you."

However, as we walked slowly back down to the fountain, Fraco stopped and chatted to several friends. At the fountain, he wanted once more to pause to see the beginning of the next parade approach. This was of the *Cofradía de los Estudiantes,* and was composed of local school children, college students and youth groups, together with some adults. The ages of the participants ranged therefore from about six to sixty.

It was well past 3 am when we finally reached Fraco's lorry and headed home. When we arrived in the village he insisted on running

175

me home, about a 10 minute drive into the *campo*. He dropped me at home at about 4.30 am, and headed back to the pueblo.

The next morning when we met in the village, he told me that as it was nearly 5 am when he reached his house, he had had some breakfast and then went straight out to milk his goats. There is something in the Spanish temperament that seems to cope with no sleep for a night or two at fiestas, seemingly without any effect. Perhaps it is because they are brought up from the earliest age in this environment. Whatever the reason, the next morning when we met up and went to a bar for a coffee just before lunch, whilst I was only half awake despite four or five hours sleep, Fraco was wide awake and lively.

CHAPTER 20

SEDELLA EN FIESTAS
(The Summer Fiesta)

One Friday evening, at the beginning of August, we had been down to Torre del Mar to do some shopping. In the afternoon the shops open from about half past five until eight or nine o'clock, and so by the time we had finished it was late, so we stopped to eat in the town before returning home. We drove back in the dark and by about eleven that night were nearing the village from the direction of Canillas de Aceituno. As we rounded a bend, about two kilometres from the pueblo, we saw in front of us in the distance a dazzling sight. Shaped like a circus big top, and seemingly hung in the dark void, was a blazing array of lights. It was the *recinto ferial,* fiesta site, of Sedella just outside the village. As we turned another corner in the winding road that runs corniche-like along the side of the mountain, the spectacle was hidden from view again by the shoulder of the hill, to reappear once more as we turned yet another corner.

Sedella was *'en fiesta'* and tonight was the first night of the three day event. When we returned to the pueblo after calling in at home to leave our shopping, it was nearly midnight. The night's entertainment was by now well underway. We parked the car and walked up to the fiesta site, which was full of people and pulsating to the music of the band playing on one of the two concrete stages at the far end. Turning up the slope on to the area itself, we met Salva Serrano who was also just arriving.

"Come for a drink," he invited us and headed to the first of the *chiringuitos,* bars, which are erected for the fiesta. This bar was being run by people from Arenas, another village some way away, and did not have many customers. There are usually four *chiringuitos* on the site and the ones that get most custom, early in the evening, are those belonging to locals. The ones that are run by 'outsiders' only fill up as the crowds grow larger later in the night.

After we had finished our drink, Salva said, "Come on, we'll go to the next bar. I always have one drink at each bar on the first night."

We went with him to the next one, which was tended by Antonio Mellado and Chachi, both local characters, and had more clients. When I tried to pay for the round Salva, having bought the first, would not let me. "I invited you," he stated firmly. This is a familiar response of the locals, if they invite you for a drink, they insist on paying for all of them. I protested in vain that he had already bought the drinks at the last bar. No, he was adamant this one was on him too.

Once again, when we had finished, he wanted to move on to the next bar which was on the other side of the site. This bar was also in the hands of locals, this time of Salva and Ani, and so once more was well attended. Salva pushed his way to the front and ordered three more wines. After a while, when we had nearly finished them, I told Wendy to distract him and keep him busy. Salva is a *caballero,* horseman, and often argues with Wendy on the respective merits of the horse and the mule. Whilst they were busy talking, I went up to the bar and paid for the drinks. When we had finished them and Salva went up to pay, he was amazed and amused that I had got in first. We were spared the fourth bar of the tour as he then got into conversation with a friend, and forgot all about his claim to always have a drink in each bar on the first night of the fiesta.

We wandered away to listen to the group and join in the dancing at the front of the stage. At about one in the morning, the group left for a break and a flamenco singer took over on the second stage. Around half past three, we left and went home, the entertainment would however continue through the night until dawn, as it would on all three nights of the fiesta.

Each town or pueblo has a patron saint, in the case of Sedella San Anton Abad, and also a Virgin with a special name or title. Canillas, for instance, has *La Virgen de la Pila*, the Virgin of the Fountain. There are Virgins of the sea, the mountain, of pity and many more besides. The Sedella fiesta lasts for three days over the first weekend of August, and is in *honor de su Patrona La Virgen de la Esperanza,* in honour of its Patron the Virgin of Hope.

On Friday, the first day, in the morning the streets of the village are hung with bunting and the lights and streamers on the *recinto* are completed. These decorations on the fiesta site itself run from numerous poles, about three metres high, set all around the perimeter to the top of a central mast. When on the *recinto* at night, covered and surrounded by these lights and bunting, it is as if you are standing in a large marquee. It was this spectacle we saw across the valley as we neared the village that Friday night.

On the following morning at about half past nine, we heard the sound of rockets being launched from the village. Going outside we looked across from our finca towards the pueblo and saw two bright flashes in the sky, quickly replaced by white puffs of smoke, and then a couple of seconds later we heard the reports as the rockets exploded. This was the wake up call to the villagers, and a warning that in about half an hour the first event of the day would occur. As this was *a pasacalle,* a walk through the streets by the band, Wendy, who plays flute in the band, had to change into her uniform and drive into the village.

During this *pasacalle,* the band collects *cintas,* tapes, from many of the houses in the pueblo. These *cintas* are coloured cloth ribbons about two inches wide, on which the girls and young women of the village embroider patterns. They are then rolled up around a cardboard tube and pinned in place with the end hanging loose, and in which is stitched a small brass ring, like a curtain ring. During the weekend, there will be two *cinta* 'races', one on bikes for the children, and the other on mule or horseback for the adults. The aim is for the riders to pass under a wire suspended above their heads on which the *cintas* have been threaded, and try to spear them through the rings with short sticks. The one who manages to pull off most tapes, which unroll and come off the tube, gets a prize and a cup. In addition to this prize, some of the tapes have banknotes fixed to them. Historically, the young men of the village would try to win the one stitched by his *novia,* girlfriend and win not just the tape but a kiss from her.

Later on in the morning, whilst the older men of the village meet in Rafa's bar to hold a domino tournament, competing for a trophy, the

179

children mount their bikes for the first *cinta*. About twenty youngsters formed up in the street, and one by one rode under the wire, reaching up to hook down a tape. All ages take part, and the wire is raised and lowered depending on the height of the contestant. The youngest this year is Noelia, daughter of Salva and Rosi of Rafa's bar, who is about three and is riding a small bike with stabilisers. She is push started by her father, who walks behind her keeping her course straight, and helping her along. As she reaches up to try and get a *cinta*, he has to duck under the wire. When a rider managers to hook a tape, it unrolls from its tube and flies out behind them as they ride past. Each successful attempt is greeted with cheers from the watching crowd, and any near miss acclaimed by jeers or groans. The biggest cheer of all comes when, almost on her last run, with only two or three *cintas* left to be won, Noelia finally manages to spear one and rides beaming up to her mother, with it trailing behind her. Two or three of the young teenagers in the race have been seriously trying to win the event and have managed to spear quite a few tapes, whilst many of the younger ones have also managed to gain one or two. When the last *cinta* is hooked off the wire, the three with the most tapes, now worn like bandoliers over one shoulder, are each given a cash prize and a silver trophy to record the event. All the contestants receive a medallion to show they have been in the race.

Another Saturday morning event is the 'marathon' races. There are two of these, the first for the very young and the second for anyone over the age of twelve. The younger children run through the village and back along the main road twice, whilst the older ones take a longer route and run it three times. August in the pueblo is a very hot month, and to attempt this race of several kilometres in the high twenties centigrade is no joke. On each circuit of the race, the runners pass the village fountain under which each dips his head to cool down. Once more there are serious contenders in each age group, cheered on by their friends and family as they run past. As at the *cinta*, both cash and trophies are to be won. There are also those, especially in the senior race, who just run for the fun of it. The winner of the adult race this year is Miguel, eldest son of our neighbour (also Miguel), with Antonio, his second eldest, in third place. Farli, the third eldest, had already won the junior race, so it was a good year for their family. Bringing up the rear, as he does every year, is Ignacio. He is in his twenties, an engineer who lives and works near Cádiz, but whose family live in the village. He and two friends of about the same age, José, who now manages the olive co-op, and Antonio, who works in the town hall, have run in the race for the last few years, usually bringing up the rear. Ignacio is cheered home as he finishes long after the winner, who in fact had lapped him on his second time round. He receives a special prize as last man.

There are many more activities on both Saturday and Sunday, for young and old alike. These include five-a-side football matches. On one of the days, there will be a series of matches between local youth teams and then for the older players, singles versus married. On the second day, a competition will be held between local villages, the winning village receiving a cup. Most of the local fiestas (and all the pueblos have a summer fiesta) will hold their own inter-village competition, with the host side always striving to win their own cup.

During the day in the *salon,* a couple of clowns or a theatre group will put on a children's show, and as most of it is done by mime or is slapstick, I can sometimes follow what is happening. If not, I can always go across the square into one of the two bars to fill in the time. At fiestas in the village that last all day, we have to plan our movements carefully. Wendy has to go in and out at the times the band is playing, and one of us has to be at the finca when it's mule feeding time. We have also to return to eat or else try to get a table in a bar, which are all busy at fiesta weekends, as well as being in the right place at the right time for all the events. Usually the times in the programme bear little relation to the time things take place, so this is not always as easy as it might seem. There are some *extranjeros,* foreigners, locally amongst the expats that live here, who tell us that they don't go to the fiesta any more as 'they have been once and seen it'. This reminds me of a boyfriend of one of our friends in England who said it was impossible to read a book more than once as 'you know what happens and how it ends'. Both of us read books again, often several times, and we always go to the fiestas. Whilst they may always follow a similar pattern, they are also always different, and in any case they are enjoyable. They are also, of course, a major social event in the life of a pueblo.

The *cinta* on animals is always worth watching. This takes place in Sedella on Sunday afternoon, in the road next to the *Ermita,* old church. During the event the band, positioned above the road on the cobbled area in front of the *Ermita,* play *pasodobles.* There are contestants on horses and mules, and sometimes even one on a donkey. Many of the younger men take the event very seriously. Once again, they are competing not just for the ribbons, but for silver cups and trophies, as well as cash and kudos. They are no longer trying to win the *cinta* decorated by their *novia,* and in any case many of the contestants are married. This year, Rafa Bravo has entered on his grey mare, resplendent in grey and black striped trousers with red braces, a white frilly shirt and grey Córdoba hat. Fermin, who takes his goats out past our finca, has entered on his donkey, other local entries include Antonio and Salva on their horses, and Salva Peales on his mule. There are also several more locals, and two or three others who have brought their animals from nearby villages. These are the serious entries, whilst others join in who are not so intent on winning, or who have no chance of doing so. Antonio Mellado, for example, who has been up for two nights running his bar on the *recinto,* and who is not quite awake or sober, is on his mule. After one or two attempts, he half falls off and Rafa Redondo mounts in his place. Wearing a huge grin, he trots under the wire vainly trying to snag a *cinta.* The pace is fast, each animal galloping under the wire and then circling the *Ermita* to try again. Every time a *cinta* is hooked, the rider is brought back, so that the girl who embroidered it can pin it round his shoulders. All the time the band play, and every time they stop cries of *'música, música'* come from the crowd. Pepe Sánchez, whose son Sergio is riding their mule, regularly leaves his place in the band and comes forward to watch the contest. When he does this, the band is without any cymbals.

Watching the *cinta,* I am reminded, when Antonio nearly falls off, of last year at the *cinta* in Salares during their fiesta. Fraquito, who lives there and who we know quite well, was riding a horse we had not seen before. He is in his sixties but a good horseman, who has been riding since he was a child. Nevertheless, he seemed to be having some trouble controlling his animal. In Salares, the *cinta* takes place not on the level, but on the road going uphill out of the village. The contestants ride up the slope first and then turn and gallop back down, each time trying to win a *cinta,* the downhill runs being quite fast. It was, fortunately, during one of the uphill runs when he was not going so fast, that Fraquito's saddle slipped and he fell into the road close to where we were standing. The horse charged off with the saddle under its belly, to be eventually caught by another contestant. Later, when we chatted to him, he told us that he had only bought the horse the day before and was not yet used to it, in fact the first time he had ridden it was for the *cinta.* He found when tacking it up that his saddle was not a good fit!

For the three nights of the fiesta, the centre of attraction is the *recinto.* This is a fairly new innovation which has been built for just a few years, or perhaps I should say is still being constructed, as new improvements are made each year as funds allow. At present, it is a large concrete area with two permanent stages at one end, with changing rooms for the entertainers. In the centre is an electric mast, and on the sides are water supply points and fixings for the metal frames that are erected to support the cane roofs, which shade the four *chiringuitos*. The development of this site has resulted in the growth of the Sedella fiesta. The custom has always been for those working away from the village, others who lived here but who have emigrated to a town to find work, and for the families of villagers, all to return to the pueblo for the weekend. In this way, the population can at least treble for a few days. The growth of the event also now brings in many people from neighbouring towns and villages each evening, an influx that generates revenue for the pueblo as well as ensuring a good weekend's entertainment for the locals. It is under the inspiration of the mayor, Francisco Gálvez Márquez, or Paco as he is known, that the fiesta has grown. He has done a lot to develop the pueblo and bring in visitors, tourists and new inhabitants, both Spanish and foreign. As a small remote *campo* village, Sedella had been for years in slow decline, as more and more locals left to work elsewhere. In recent years, however, this decline has been stemmed, and a slow but steady growth has started to replace it.

With the exception of the fireworks display on Sunday evening, which takes place at the *Ermita*, all the night time activity takes place at the *recinto*. Each evening, a group will play on one stage for long periods, whilst specialist acts use the second one. This year, we had the flamenco singer on the Friday and on Sunday a quite well-known Spanish pop group. The presence of a prominent pop group, a different one each year, draws in crowds of teenagers from miles around. On the Saturday evening this year, the special attraction was Alicia Fernández. Her family were originally from the village, and she has many relatives still here. She is a vocalist in the flamenco style, but with a more modern slant. She is popular in the pueblo and has written a song about the village which she always sings, and which of course is a favourite with everyone.

The fiesta, being in August, always enjoys good weather. Until about forty years ago it was held in May, but was changed for a variety of reasons. Salva Peales, father of the one riding in the *cinta,* explained to us one day that the weather was more reliable in August than May and the nights warmer. August too, he said, being a holiday month, made it easier for those living or working in other parts of Spain or Europe to return for the event. Lastly, he said that those still living in Sedella and, like himself, working long hours in the *campo*, were less busy in August than May, and so not so tired and could enjoy it more. This year, however, the mayor introduced a new fiesta in May on the day of '*La Virgen de la Esperanza*' when the original fiesta used to be. This was a *romería,* and was situated at the new camp site, another of the mayor's innovations, and included a barbeque. As Salva had predicted, it rained, not a usual occurrence in May, so we look forward to the coming May to see what happens then.

Last year, as I stood on the recinto at about two o'clock in the morning, surrounded by hundreds of people amid a sea of noise and pop music, I looked around. The bars were full; the area was filled with the old, the very young and all ages in between; there were stalls selling *turron,* nuts, sweets and candy floss; there was a bouncy castle, a children's roundabout and dodgems; stalls were selling chicken, hamburgers and *churros,* a fried batter; couples walked past with babies in pushchairs; children were running everywhere and old men leaning on walking sticks stood gazing about them. I thought about the remarks of an English acquaintance, who lived near the village, who had complained about the noise and expense of the fiesta. "Of course, the old people don't like them," she had said. "They're too noisy for them, too many rockets and loud music." I walked across to Manolo, our elderly neighbour of over 80, who was standing nearby. Manolo has a house in the *campo* near ours, and also one in the village. He values the quiet of the *campo* and prefers living out there, rather than staying in the pueblo.

"The music's a bit loud, isn't it?" I tried out on him.

He looked at me blankly. "Loud?" he questioned. "Of course it's loud, it's a fiesta!" He, like everyone else, old or young, was enjoying the night. Which old people, I thought, don't like the noise? None that I knew.

What was for certain was that most of the locals would still be here after I had gone home to get some sleep. Tomorrow, or rather today, Monday, is a *fiesta local,* a local day of rest, when the village can sleep in and recover from the long weekend. But for now Sedella is *'en fiesta'.*

CHAPTER 21

MI PUEBLO HOY

(My village today)

The village today, 22 years after I first moved here, is of course substantially the same as it was then. However, there have also been many changes in both its physical appearance and in the lifestyles of its inhabitants.

Let us approach the pueblo once again from the west, on the road from Canillas de Aceituno. The first thing that can be seen is that the hostal, Casa Pinta, is closed. It is at present in the hands of the receivers, and so will no doubt in time be sold off and reopened. For now, however, it is closed. At the bend, to the right the *recinto ferial,* fiesta site, has been enlarged and above it the sports area now has a swimming pool, tennis and paddle courts, and a bar as well alongside the football pitch. Beyond the *recinto* on the left of the track is a large olive mill that has replaced the old one in the village. This also, unfortunately, has been closed for a few years owing to the reduction in the number of people working in the *campo* and also in the rapid acquisition of cars by the remainder, allowing them to take their olives further afield to be sold, presumably at a better price.

The two bars on the right of the main road, Bar Andaluz and Bar Granada, are also closed and both are now private dwellings.

The road into the village as it branches into the pueblo is now a building site, as it is being completely revamped. Soon however, say in a few months, it will be finished and provide a fine entrance for visitors. On the left of this road is now a small tourist office.

The square above this road on the left has been completely redeveloped. The row of buildings along the north side have all been demolished and a large new *ayuntamiento,* town hall, has been constructed in their place, with a new doctor's surgery incorporated into it on the ground floor. The washhouses alongside have been given a facelift, and the room above is now the meeting place for the Women's Group. Where the old olive mill was situated on the other

186

side of the road, there stands a large Visitor Centre for the National Park, with a museum and exhibition centre. In this building are a gym and the village Guadalinfo, an internet access centre. The old town hall inside the village is now used by various groups for meetings, exhibitions, classes and the like.

As you walk though the village, it is obvious that most of the houses have been renovated as have the smaller *calles*. Some of these improvements are still ongoing. The church and the *salon* next to it appear much the same, but inside they too have had a facelift. The result of all this modernisation is that the village looks smarter and up to date, and not still in the nineteenth century as it appeared when I first came. For the tourist, it no doubt looks less quaint and picturesque, but for the inhabitants it is a far nicer place to live. And despite the changes, it is still attractive and striking, and typical of the *pueblos blancos* of the region, and has retained its *Mudéjar* style.

At the far end of the left hand road through the village, two old council houses have been demolished near the *Ermita*, and there is now a large cleared space where a new school may be built.

In the hollow between the two village streets, the beautiful and productive stand of avocado trees have been chopped down and replaced by a large new private house, and further on up the right hand side of the valley is a new road that rises up the side along which are more new houses. Along the lane to the Roman bridge, even more have been built and indeed here and there all round the village perimeter. The rapid growth of houses in the surrounding *campo* has however largely dried up, as the rules on building in the countryside have been both made more stringent and enforced more effectively.

The small village shop near the old town hall has now been closed, but a new one has opened and can be found where the two village streets split. The store near the church is still in existence but is one general store and not a separate bread shop, grocers and fishmongers. The second bar in the square by the church, *Un Poquito Más*, has closed whilst Bar Plaza, despite changing hands several times, is still there.

Frasco Miguel is no longer a goatherd and has opened a new bar 'Meson Frasco' in part of his house, which he now rents out. It is opposite the new shop near the branch in the village street.

These then are the main physical changes to the pueblo, there have been many more which may not be too obvious to people walking through the streets, but which have had profound effects.

One striking change is the growth in car ownership. When I first came to the pueblo, only one or two locals owned cars. All the *extranjeros,* foreigners, did of course, but most of them like me lived in the *campo*. All transporting of crops from the land to the village was done by mule, or in a few cases by donkey. When I first came here, Wendy and I used to throw a party once a year, mainly for the local Spanish. When we held the first one, we didn't appreciate that transport would be a problem. We live about 1½ kilometres from the village, and so for that first one an English friend who lived in the area and had a transit van ran a shuttle service to and fro, to bring the less mobile elderly people out to our finca, and then take them home at the end. The rest of the locals walked both ways, as they were used to walking around the village to get to their land, and it didn't bother them at all. Over about six or seven years all this changed, and most families came out in their own cars. The track above our house became one large car park.

This growth in car ownership has led to the dramatic reduction in the number of mules in the village, the transporting of crops now being carried out by cars. When I first came to the pueblo, there were more than 50 mules in the village, and now they can be counted on the fingers of one hand. There is still the odd donkey and several horses, but the total of equines as a whole has been decimated.

Another change has been the reduction in the number of herds of goats and, more significantly, the closure of the goat sheds within the village itself and the building of new ones around it in the *campo*.

These two changes have resulted in the removal of animals using the village streets. This means of course that there are no longer droppings underfoot, but this increase in hygiene is, in my opinion, not of sufficient benefit to balance against the loss of seeing the animals passing in the streets.

During my time here, the village has also had a growing number of *extranjeros* moving into it. Many British and northern Europeans have arrived, together with successive waves of Moroccans, Poles and Rumanians. Whilst the Brits and the northern Europeans have mainly stayed here, the others have reduced in number leaving only a few of each behind. This influx of immigrants, myself included, has inevitably changed the nature of the village somewhat, although it remains overwhelmingly Spanish.

Together however with the slow down in the number of young people leaving the village to go and work in places such as Málaga, Granada, Sevilla and elsewhere, this has altered the demographics. With the ability to travel to local towns to work, more young Spanish couples have married and stayed in the village. These two factors have resulted in an increase in children in the pueblo, both Spanish and foreigners. When I first came here, the village school had only a handful of children and was in danger of closure. The increase in children living in the village swelled the numbers, and led both to an increase in teachers and plans to build a new school. Now, however, things have gone backwards to a certain extent, and the school numbers have fallen off as the 'bulge' has now gone on to secondary school in Cómpeta, and the plans for a new school are in doubt. Time will tell where the numbers will stabilise.

This then is the pueblo today, still growing and changing, as of course it always will. I cannot draw a neat line under it and say "this is what it was and this is what it is now". As I have described, many of the changes are ongoing and today's given will one day in its turn belong to history.

So this book should perhaps more properly be called 'Sedella: The Ongoing Story of a Village'.

BIBLIOGRAPHY

BOOKS WHOSE READING HAS BEEN INSTRUMENTAL IN WRITING THIS STORY

The Story of Spain by Mark Williams. Mirador Books
A History of Islamic Spain by W Montgomery Watt and Pierre Cachia. Edinburgh University Press
La Ruta Blanca del Mudéjar by Manuel Fernández Mota. A Mazuelo, Algeciras
Franco by Sheelagh Elllwood. Longman, London & New York
The Face of Spain by Gerald Brennan. Penguin Books
South from Granada by Gerald Brennan. Penguin Books
The Spanish Labyrinth by Gerald Brennan. Cambridge University Books
A Rose for Winter by Laurie Lee. Vintage Books. London

65975921R00105

Made in the USA
Charleston, SC
13 January 2017